To: YY

Bent

A Destinations Novel

N. Dennis

Bent by: S. H. Timmins

COPYRIGHT © 2015 BY S. H. Timmins

All rights reserved.

Editing by: Neeley Bratcher

Cover Design by: S. H. Timmins

Photo: Stock Photography

Without limiting the rights under copyright reserved above, no part of this publication may be reproduced, stored in or introduced into a retrieval system, or transmitted, in any form, or by any means (electronic, mechanical, photocopying, recording, or otherwise) without the prior written permission of both the copyright owner of the above publisher of this book.

This is a work of fiction. Names, characters, places, brands, media, and incidents are either the product of the author's imagination or are used fictitiously. The author acknowledges the trademarked status and trademark owners of various products, bands, and/or restaurants referenced in this work of fiction, have been used without permission. The publication/use of

these trademarks is not authorized, associated with, or sponsored by the trademark owners.

This book is dedicated to the memory of my mother.

Prologue

My name is Alex Bradley. I had a good life, with friends, a job that I loved, and women. One night, it all changed.

They call me, "The Puddle Maker." The name was given to me by my two best friends. They say it's because every time I walk into a room, women drool and wet their panties, creating a puddle. I've never seen any evidence to support this claim, and believe me, I've looked. Now, if I am The Puddle Maker, then my friends are, "The Bad Boy," and "God's Gift to Women." Dante, The Bad Boy, draws women to him by some unseen magnet, and then charms the underwear right off of them. I think it has to do with

this whole buffed, biker image he has that draws them in, but it is the teddy bear inside of him that has them giving up their honey. Now Logan, God's Gift to Women, is the real whopper of our trio. If women could build an altar to him, they would, and some probably have. He can make even the most intelligent of women become fan girls in his orbit, throwing their panties at him and fainting. I have to admit, the guy is a god among mere me I own one of the hottest nightclubs in the country with my friends, and I make a decent amount of money while doing it. We came up with the idea one drunken night in college. Don't all the greatest ideas happen while drinking? Each of us has very specific skill sets, but when we put those skills together, genius happens. I have a Master's in Business Management, Dante is a whiz with computers, and has an Engineering Degree to back his skills, and Logan is an Accountant, and gets disturbingly excited by numbers. The great idea? It was to open a club that was a technological heaven. We have computerized walls that transport you to anywhere in the world with climate control to accessorize the scenery for a more authentic feel. Each week, we choose a different location. Some are tourist attractions, some are exotic, and some are obscure. The allure is this: who doesn't want to travel to places around the world? We coordinate the food and drinks, even the outfits that the staff wear are chosen to compliment that week's theme.

Brilliant, right?

So what happened, you want to know?

I have named it, "The Incident." It was an event that changed my life forever.

This is my story...

Chapter One

I'm coming out of the office, when Dante stops me. He is also our Head of Security, as well as overseeing all of the computers. I don't like the look on his face. When Dante is worried about something, he looks constipated. I'm looking at constipated.

"What's the problem?"

"Logan hasn't shown up yet, and he isn't answering his cell."

Rolling my eyes, I tell him, "He is probably getting laid." Which is usually true.

Dante eyes me stoically and says, "He is never late when Laney is working."

True, and highly amusing. Laney seems to have

an anti-god gene. She is the only woman that we know of who doesn't have an altar dedicated to Logan. She sees him as the mere mortal that he really is.

It. Drives. Him. Insane.

He is determined to bring her over to *The Dark Side* and makes a complete ass of himself in his pursuit of this goal.

Priceless.

I reluctantly agree that this seems out of character for Logan. He is diligent in his pursuit of Laney, and he is usually here long before she is scheduled to work. I am starting get a bad feeling, like a foreboding of impending doom.

I should have listened to my gut that night.

"Give him a few more minutes, and if he still isn't here, I will send out, The Bat Signal."

We don't actually have a Bat Signal. It's our nickname for the emergency signal that Dante has programmed into all of our phones. If he doesn't answer our emergency signal, then I will have to go to his "Pleasure Pad" and see what's wrong. Yes, Pleasure Pad is a nickname for his apartment, but not one that we gave it. That honor would fall on the lovely heads of all the women who have had a divine experience at the aforementioned Pleasure Pad.

Enough said.

Giving a tight nod, Dante turns around and walks back towards the bar area where the girls are gearing up for the night.

Our staff has an equal ratio of males to females and there is a shift leader for each gender. The instruction session for our girls is more of a pep-rally speech before the big game. The boys have a speech more along the lines of what you would hear in the locker room.

Each have important roles to play here, but there is a difference. Our girls take a lot more harassment than our guys, and therefore have to be more careful. Part of their speech before a shift is to go over all the safety procedures that we have in place for them. Dante takes their safety very seriously, and I am sure he is hero-worshipped for it by most of them. Don't get me wrong, we all value our employees, but Dante is the 'Knight-In-Shining-Armor' for them. Our boys get harassed too, but somehow there are very few complaints, and not a single safety protocol has been needed. Go figure.

I stand at the end of the bar, and observe the room. Tonight is a tropical destination theme. We have the walls reflecting a sunset beach which, because it is computerized, has waves gently lapping against powdery white sand, and even birds flying in the distance. There is a warm breeze blowing through the club via our climate control system, and a light flowery fragrance scents the air, with a hint of fresh fruits. The girls are wearing toga-style mini-dresses with a vivid floral pattern in hues of blue and gold. The guys have on Hawaiian-style shirts in the same pattern over cargo shorts. The whole effect is a tropical paradise.

I feel my phone vibrate in my pocket. Once I retrieve it, I quickly glance at the screen. I see that it is Logan sending a text, and open it immediately. It reads that he is on his way, and will explain when he gets here. I have that sense of impending doom again.

Damn gut.

Finally, an hour later, Logan arrives. I notice that he isn't quite as impeccable as usual. He still draws every female head in the club, but he isn't dressed like he usually is. Instead of one of his expensive suits, he is dressed in jeans and a button-down shirt. Not his usual attire at the club when we're open. I'm so distracted by the state that Logan is in that I don't notice the vision standing beside him. If Logan is *God's Gift to Women*, then this would be his female equivalent. She has long, dark hair and amazing, sapphire-blue eyes. This hourglass figure that is wrapped in skinny jeans and a soft, pink sweater, hugging succulent breasts. And these lips that look almost pornographic in their plumpness. I get hard so fast, that I feel a bit light-headed. I finally notice the lack of noise in my immediate area, and reluctantly pull my gaze away from the scrumptious view before me. Every man and woman has stopped what they are doing, and is standing, transfixed by the couple before me. I must admit, they just made the world more beautiful, or at least our little corner of it. I blink to clear my vision, and try looking back at my friend. He is grabbing the back of his neck and squeezing, an obvious sign of distress for him. Immediately, I am on alert. Logan would never show any sign of weakness or emotion in public.

"The office?" I offer, and jerk my head in that direction.

Logan lets out a sigh and walks past me, leading the way. I turn to the heavenly creature and indicate with my arm that she should precede me. She walks past me and I, in turn, follow behind. I try not to notice her ass, I really do, but it is like my gaze it drawn there against my will. Okay, it wasn't against my will, I willingly eye-hump her ass. It is a stellar ass, and as a card-carrying member of *The Man Club*, I am duty bound to appreciate her ass.

Once all of us are inside the office, I shut the door. The silence is like a cocoon. Someone needs to breathe a bit heavier, or crack a knuckle, scuff the carpet, anything. I take a deep breath, prepared to be the first to break the silence, when Logan speaks first.

"Call Dante. This concerns him as well."

I try to read the look on Logan's face, but honestly I have no idea what he is thinking. I chance a glance at the goddess, but she is looking at all the monitors in the room that are showing various angles around the club. I grab my phone from my pocket and send a quick text off to Dante, instructing him to come to the office. I put my phone back, and look up at Logan. He is watching the Beauty. Before I have a chance to ask him what this is all about, Dante knocks on the door and enters. As he walks in and shuts the door, all eyes go to him, including Ms. Luscious.

Damn. I really need to find out what her name is or I am going to run out of descriptive words.

Dante sucks in a breath when he sees her. I can sympathize with how the sight of her must be impacting him. Suddenly, the angel (I really need to find out her name) squeals and launches herself at him.

Wait a minute. What did I miss?

"Oh God, Dante. It has been too long!" She is wrapped around him at this point. There isn't a hope of even a pubic hair squeezing between them.

"Pumpkin, what are you doing here?"

Dante called her...Pumpkin?

Am I in *The Twilight Zone*?

Seriously, what am I missing here?

"*Pumpkin* showed up on my doorstep last night, looking for a job."

The fact that Logan said the word "pumpkin" in the same tone you would say a dog's name alerts me to the fact that Logan isn't happy about this. Dante looks over Pumpkin's head, and gives Logan an eloquent look that speaks volumes.

Wait! Does he mean she wants to work here?

Oh, hell yes!

"Why do you need a job?" Dante doesn't sound any happier than, Logan.

I have had enough of this shit! Time to remind everyone that I am in the room, and clueless.

"Hi there, Pumpkin. I don't think that we have met before. I am Alex, and I would love to have you as part of the team." I smile with all my "puddle-making" ability.

Dante immediately releases Pumpkin and whirls around shooting me a look filled with retribution. Logan doesn't waste his time with a look. He shoots me verbally.

"First of all, Alex, you don't have all the facts. Second, you have met before. Pumpkin is better known as, Shay. My cousin, Shayla."

WTF?

Shay? As in, little Shayla, his baby cousin, that used to have acne, and wear braces?

I take a closer look. Her hair was always frizzy, whereas now it lies in sleek waves. She used to be a little chubby, but now the only thing chubby in this room is in my pants. After a very thorough perusal, from tits to toes, I take a closer look above the chest. That is when I see it. I was so blinded by her beauty that I didn't really look close enough. It is in her eyes that I can see the child she was and the woman she has become. Really though, with so much to ogle, I can't be held accountable for my lack of attention to detail. I mentioned *The Man Card*, right? I rest my case.

She smirks me. This is also when I realize that she has stood there while I just eye-fucked her. I feel a like a pervert and I open my mouth to apologize, but she waves her hand at me.

"Honestly, Alex, it is okay. I have changed a lot, and it has been years since we have seen each other. I have seen Dante the odd time through the years because he does some computer work for my dad. Really, don't feel bad. I did recognize you." Here she licks her lips, and takes her time checking me out, from hair to hard-on. "Although, you have filled out a lot from the young man I remember."

Damn, is anyone else hot in here?

I think I was just sized up like a juicy steak. She is biting her lip now, like she wants to bite something else.

Does anyone have any barbeque sauce?

"Okay, now that we are all reacquainted, let's get to the reason why Shay wants a job. She is working for a small magazine that wants her to write an article on how and why men objectify women." Logan looks at both Dante, and me. "She feels that if she were to become one of our serving girls, that she would find a 'gold mine' of information."

"Hang on, Logan. You are making it sound far worse than it is. I just want the opportunity to speak with some of the girls, and even the guys, and experience for myself how hard it is to do a job and be professional while dealing with these issues. It is a serious injustice in our society that affects women and men who are trying to make a living. I am not saying that your club is a horrible place to work, quite the opposite. I know how safe you keep your employees, and that is the main reason why I came to you instead of another club."

Well, there is that. Logan looks like his head might pop like a zit, while Dante looks thoughtful. I know that Logan always felt more like a brother to Shay. I almost pity him right now...almost.

My dick likes the idea of having her around. I tend to agree with it.

Logan groans and then hangs his head. When he looks up, I can tell he has made a decision.

"Okay, Shay, here is how it is going to go down. We will officially hire you for a temporary position. You will work two nights a week, but you will do everything that we tell you, and you do not tell anyone here that you are working on a paper."

Shay squeals again, but this time launches herself at Logan. He enfolds her in a tender hug, and whispers into her ear. Whatever he says, she nods enthusiastically, and then whispers something back. Logan lets her go, and she walks towards Dante. She reaches up and wraps her arms around our *Bad Boy* in a warm hug. Dante returns the hug and tells her that he will see her soon. Finally, it is my turn. She turns, smiles a secret smile, and then walks towards me. I loosen my limbs, preparing for all that soft, squishy goodness to be pressed against me. My dick starts to perk back up and gives a jaunty salute from my pants. She gets closer, and the smell of warm woman invades my personal space. Just as I am about to reach for her, she veers off-course at the last second. I stand there, stunned, as she passes me and proceeds to open the door and walk through it, closing it behind her.

Did that just happen?

I glare at Logan, knowing he had something to do with it.

He glares back.

It is on!

Dante clears his throat. "I need to get back to the floor. I'll talk to you guys later."

I don't really notice him leave the room. The glare-off is still going on. Logan, cracks first. He takes a deep breath and looks at the wall, instead of me, when he starts talking.

"You are one of my best friends, and we are as close as brothers. We know each other better than anyone. She deserves better than us. Dante is a non-issue as there has never been anything but a kind of affection between them. What I saw on your face when you were looking at her was lust in in its rawest form. Now, I told her and I am telling you, she is here as an employee. She is not to become involved with any of the staff, and that includes you, Puddle-Maker."

Chapter Two

Needless to say, I don't handle the order well. After some yelling (Logan) and some crying (me), we come to an understanding. I have to agree that I am a man-whore, and I'm not interested in her personality. I just want her body, and I'm thinking only what I could do with it. Since Logan shares my inclinations towards women, this wasn't shocking to him. It does, however, enlighten me to how I might feel if I had a cousin/sister. I'm still not happy about his decision, the cock-blocker, but I can respect it, for now.

After we say all that we need to on the matter, I leave the office to make my rounds on the floor. Logan says he needs to stay in the office and get her paperwork started. He also needs to draw up a non-disclosure contract for her to sign so that she can't use our club name or any staff names in her article.

I perch at my usual spot by the bar. Our bar is really a work of art. The bar counter takes up an entire wall and needs a staff of six to run it. The bar itself is an actual fish tank with a glass counter.

Genius, right?

It is a huge draw, and one of our best features. We have a sunken dance floor in the middle of the room, and a circular floor surrounding it with lounging chairs and low coffee tables. It creates a lounge-like feel with a club vibe. There is the main entrance off to the right where Dante and his security staff check I.D.'s and control the flow in and out of the club. We also have security in the main room and down the halls off to the left that lead to the rest rooms. There are two separate hallways for the bathrooms, one for men and one for women. This was a safety decision that has worked out very well for us. At the back of the main room is a closed-off hallway that leads to the computer rooms and security rooms. Behind the bar, we have our last corridor which leads to our office, the staff rooms, and our kitchen. Our kitchen is used to make appetizers that we coordinate to match our themes. We are not a restaurant, but we wanted a way to blend exotic finger foods with our bar menu. This is our dream and our life. We have been open for just over five years now, after the three grueling years we spent trying to get the club up and running.

Now I know you have been dying to know what this masterpiece is named. I won't keep you in suspense any longer.

We named our club...Destinations.

Brilliant, I know.

I was feeling a little on edge (and a lot horny) after seeing the wonder that is Shay. I need to choose a woman for the night to release some of the pressure in my balls. Having a semi for some time now is causing the boys to feel a bit swollen. I am never lacking for female attention.

That is not my ego talking. Just stating the facts.

I know that I am an attractive guy. I have been told enough. Plus, I do realize what stares back at me every day from the mirror. I stand at a height of six-foot four, which is pretty tall. I have a decently muscular build, but I'm not as defined as Logan, or as bulky as Dante. My hair is a sandy brown, which I wear longer than most guys, but not long enough for a ponytail, like Dante. My eyes are a greenish shade of hazel. As an overall package, I know the appeal that I have on the opposite sex, and unfortunately some members of the same sex. With that being said, I begin my hunt.

I spot several likely candidates that I feel would enjoy a spin around my bedroom tonight. We have a choice between a brunette and a redhead. I am leaning more towards the brunette, and I am sure that Freud could tell you why. I make my approach slowly, enjoying the reactions that I am receiving from passing females.

I still don't see any puddles but there was definitely some drool.

I see that she has noticed my approach as she turns and starts whispering to a woman beside her while eyeing me. She turns back just as I reach her table. She looks slightly dazed and yes, there is a little drool. It almost isn't fair the effect that our trio has on women...almost.

I begin the negotiations.

"Good evening, ladies. I couldn't help admiring your beauty from across the room. My name is Alex. And whom, may I ask, are you enchanting beauties?

Smooth, right?

The brunette giggles, and my eyebrows wing up.

"We know who you are, Mr. Bradley."

I pause here for a moment, and the brunette's friend notices. She nudges her in the side.

"Oh, I am so sorry, Mr. Bradley. I just meant that we know who you are, and possibly why you are here with us. My name is Kylie, and this is my friend, Trisha."

Well, it seems that I may not have to spell out

my intentions for her sexy, little body.

"Since you seem to presume why I am at your table, shall we dispense with the formalities then?"

Kylie giggles again. There is something about gigglers that just doesn't work for me. I can feel my semi shrinking, and that sense of impending disaster is back in my gut.

I should have walked away.

There must be some vibe that I am throwing out which alerts her to where my thoughts are heading. She jumps up from her spot on the lounge and plasters herself to my side without giggling.

Improvement.

"Yes. Whatever it is, my answer is, yes! Trisha can get a cab home without me, right Trish?"

Her friend nods enthusiastically towards her. I can almost feel Kylie's eagerness vibrating against me.

Maybe I will just take her upstairs to our love nest instead of my place. Yes, that sounds horrible (don't judge me), but we have had trouble with women stalking our homes in the past, and this is sometimes safer. Also, we work long hours into the night. It is really convenient to have a place to crash.

This is starting to feel like one of those times.

"I will make sure that she gets home safe,

Trisha. You have my word. If you would like to stay for a while longer, your drinks will be on me."

Wide eyed, she politely thanks me, and then turns a mischievous smile toward Kylie. I am pretty sure that was a smiling "high-five".

I gently remove Kylie from my side and put my hand on her lower back so that I can guide her.

The stairs leading to the apartment above the club are at the end of the hallway, behind the bar. I escort Kylie along the corridor until we reach the end. I punch in the security code and open the door. I indicate that she should go on ahead of me.

She giggles.

I stifle a sigh, and follow her up the stairs.

The back view is very nice, just not as nice as Shay's.

No, I shouldn't be thinking about her right now, but my brain doesn't seem to be getting the memo. As I climb the stairs, my mind seems to be playing its top five favorite parts of Shay's body on a constant loop. My dick sees this too and starts to lengthen in my pants. At least after all that giggling I am hard again.

I was getting worried.

We reach the top of the stairs and I enter another code for this door. Dante takes our security very seriously. Again, I usher her on before me. I follow behind her, and shut the door.

Alone in the apartment, with the noise from the club now a distant throb, I'm starting feel uneasy again.

What is wrong with me?

I have a gorgeous woman here with me, ready to embark on an evening of ecstasy. Giving myself a mental slap, I do the polite thing, and ask her if she would like anything.

I may be a bit of a slut, but I am a gentleman slut.

She declines, with another giggle.

I sigh, aloud this time.

She doesn't seem to notice. Her eyes are gobbling up every detail of the apartment. Feeling slightly frustrated, I place my hand at the small of her back and steer her towards the bedroom. I walk past her into the room and head for the nightstand to turn on a soft light.

Much better.

I sit on the bed, and turn to face her.

"Why don't you join me, on the bed? We can get to know each other better."

I smile for all that I am worth and bring out, The

Puddle Maker.

She seems to sway for a moment, and then slowly walks her way towards me. She delicately perches on the bed beside me. She really is quite pretty. She has rich brown eyes, a petite nose and a shy, yet alluring, smile. She is smiling at me now. I slowly lean towards her, and then stop an inch away from her lips. She seems to be holding her breath. Before we take this to the next level, I need to allow her the chance to change her mind.

See? A gentleman slut.

"Kylie, you are a very beautiful woman. I would be honored if you will allow me the pleasure of your body. I can promise that the pleasure will be mutual, and I will respect your decision, either way."

She lets out a tiny puff of air, followed by a deep sigh. She whispers the word, "Yes," against my lips, and that is the only confirmation that I need.

Game on!

Chapter Three

The events that follow will forever be known as, "The Incident."

I will fast forward through the preliminaries and get right to the main event.

As far as sexual experiences go, it isn't horrible, but I am having trouble staying fully engaged.

Fine, I'm having trouble maintaining my erection.

Let's just get something straight right now, I have NEVER had this problem before. I am always strong, like a bull, and can perform like an athlete.

Yes, this is what I have been told, but it is also a fact.

I can tell that Kylie is starting to take it

personally because she is riding me for all she is worth. The girl could ride a bronco with pride. I am murmuring sweet words of encouragement and praise to her.

I am also trying to have a mental pep talk with my dick. It isn't going too well. While I am mentally asking *The Big Guy* (my nickname for my penis, and yes, the name fits), what the problem might be, I swear I hear my dick whimper Shay's name.

Shay?

As soon as I think it, I can feel a glorious tingle in my dick. It perks up at this, begging for more, and promising results if I continue with this train of thought.

Why not? Nothing else is working.

I picture the generous swells of Shay's bountiful bosom, in that pink sweater which was hugging her breasts in a way that made me want to go motor boating. Instantly, my dick flares to life! I swear this is the hardest that I have been all night. I give a mental high five to *The Big Guy* and now I am back in the game.

Kylie seems to be pleased with the results too, if the sounds coming from her are any indication.

Shit, Kylie!

This isn't fair to her. I am having sex with her and fantasizing about another woman. I decide to concentrate on her instead, and just like that, my dick starts to deflate again. I am panicking now and penis nudges brain to get with the visual stimulation. Fantasies of Shay fill my mind. Dick preens while engorging with half the blood in body, or at least that is what it feels like. It is during this moment that Kylie decides to go for her gold medal performance. I am feeling so bad about this, and I shift to try and get her attention when the unthinkable happens.

>Now, I have to stress how horrific this is.

>Imagine the worst pain possible.

>Are you imagining it?

>Well, it isn't even close!

>There are no words for the extent of the suffering that I am about to experience.

>As I am shifting, Kylie is slamming back down on me, when it happens.

>Sorry...just give me a moment here. I still have nightmares about this, and I am having trouble reliving it.

>Alright, I am just going to say it.

>She. Broke. My. Dick.

>Yes, you read that right.

>Somehow, while she was descending, my poor penis gets bent, almost in half! Then there is this awful popping sound.

My penis...popped!

We are not talking about a little bend in the worm here either. Oh no, it was bent in half.

Bent. In. Half.

I will allow the visual to take root.

Go on, picture it.

Are you feeling my pain?

Sweet baby Jesus, it hurt!

I honestly didn't know that this was physically possible. Nothing like finding out the hard way, or not so hard as the case may be, since my erection is gone (I fear forever), and my dick is trying to retract inside me. I immediately start screaming and thrashing about on the bed. My thrashing, unfortunately, causes Kylie to be launched into the air and from astride me. I am concerned for her of course, and the fact that I managed to dislodge the condom with her, but I am having trouble staying conscious at this point. I have never felt close to passing out from pain before, but I am now. I distantly hear her asking me if I am alright. Well, at least I know that she is fine, but I am not alright and fear I may never be again.

I think I must temporarily pass out because the next thing that I know, Kylie has somehow managed to retrieve my phone from my pants pocket and she is shaking it at me. She looks panicked, and she is rambling about emergency numbers. A light bulb goes off over my head.

The Bat Signal!

Gasping and sweating while my vision is starting to swim, I manage to take the phone from her. Thank God I only have to push a single button to activate the signal because I know anything else is beyond me at this point. I need to let Kylie know that the cavalry will be arriving, but only manage gurgling sounds when I try.

I must have passed out again, because now Dante is peering down at me. I know that I have to say something, anything, to let him know what the "code red" is. I try to speak, but wheezing emerges this time. Dante turns, and says something over his shoulder to someone beyond what my vision is capable of focusing on at this point. A moment later, I hear Kylie's voice. I should be embarrassed about how this must look, but I just don't have it in me to care. More conversation is spoken, but I have tuned it out. I can't focus on anything past my pain.

Several minutes later, Dante squats down in front of me. I am looking at his constipated face for the second time this evening.

"From what I can gather, you have injured your dick while having sex. Logan is asking if we should call for an ambulance. I need for you to tell me if that is necessary."

I manage one word. "Bent."

Dante frowns. "You bent your dick? How does that even happen?"

Apparently, it happens when you are being mounted like a pommel horse at the Olympics. Maybe being ridden like a pogo stick would be more accurate? Not important right now. I girded my loins, or what is left of them, to answer Dante.

"Ambulance, yes."

Dante gives a decisive nod, and turns to whom I assume is either Kylie or Logan. I am feeling nauseous now. Dante turns back to tell me that the ambulance is on the way. He grabs one of the covers, which have ended up on the floor, and drapes it over me. Modesty is not what I am worried about, but I am grateful all the same.

☺

I am lying on a gurney in an emergency room cubicle sometime later. I have been examined, assessed, and had various tests done. Words like "penile fracture, "and "hematoma, "and "tunica albuginea, "have been said to me. I have been given some pain medication (thank God), so my cognitive abilities are slightly impaired. I am having trouble understanding all the information they are throwing at me. From what I have been able to grasp, they are telling me that I might have a small tear inside my penis, in the lining where the blood collects for erections. There is also the possibility that I can develop a blood clot. I can expect swelling and bruising as well. If it is serious enough, they will have to operate on my penis.

O. M. G!

Did you get all that?

Tears, and blood clots, and surgery.

Oh my!

This isn't happening.

I love my penis!

Logan rides with me in the ambulance, and is holding up a wall beside me. Dante stayed back at the club, since one of us needs to be there, and said that he will join us at the hospital when he's finished.

I told Dante that I don't need him to hold my hand.

He told me to kiss his ass.

I have great friends.

I am just about to attempt sitting up, when the curtain is pulled back. The doctor who has been seeing me enters the room. He seems nice enough. He is a little older than me, maybe around thirty five, with an average height and looks. He isn't a smiling doctor, but he seems to know what he is talking about, which is the important thing. He is carrying a clipboard that he is focused on at the moment. He puts the clipboard down, and looks at me. I can tell by the look on his face that I am not going to like what he is about to say.

"Mr. Bradley, according to the tests that we have run, it appears that there is a possibility of a small tear. As far as we can tell, there has been minimal bleeding. Your penis is already starting to shows signs of some swelling and bruising. There are ways that we can treat the swelling, and minimize the bruising. Unfortunately, there are only two options for the tear. One, we can send you home and instruct you to limit your activity. Abstain from sexual intercourse, including masturbation, as well as try to avoid anything that might give you an erection. I understand that an erection can happen without conscious thought or stimulation, just try to avoid what you can control. We would then see how it heals on its own. Two, we can perform a non-invasive surgical procedure, to go in and fix the tear. If you choose to avoid surgery for now, there is still a possibility that the tear may not heal properly, and surgery will still be required. The choice is yours, and we will respect your decision. For the swelling, an anti-inflammatory such as Ibuprofen may be used as needed. The bruising can be minimized with an ice pack, but do not leave it on for longer than ten minutes at a time. The ice will also help alleviate some of the swelling. The pain will begin to ease, and the Ibuprofen will help with that. Do you have any questions?"

I was right. I don't like what he has to say.

Actually, that is a gross understatement. I am horrified by what he has told me.

How the hell am I supposed to make such a life-altering decision like this?

Yes, life-altering.

Without a fully functioning penis, my way of life is completely altered.

Ask any man, he will tell you the same thing. Life without a penis is not a life. At least, not a life that I can even fathom.

I look towards Logan, hoping to get some help there, but by the look on his face, he is suffering the same thoughts.

Okay, I can do this on my own.

Surgery on my penis is not an option for me at this point. My dick has suffered through enough tonight and there is no way that I can subject him to a scalpel on top of all the trauma he has been through.

I think I just felt him shudder at the thought.

I hear ya, Big Guy.

Not. Happening.

So that leaves me with the option of going home and hoping that I have Wolverine's healing abilities where this tear is concerned.

I guess that I just made my decision then.

"I believe at this point that I will try and heal naturally. How long is the healing process?"

Please tell me it's just a few days!

"It varies for each individual, but the expected recovery time from an injury such as this would be around two weeks. If this is the course that you wish to take, I would ask that you follow up with your family doctor after the two weeks. I will write down some things that you should watch for while you are healing. If any of these things should happen, I want you to come back here right away. If you have no further questions, I will start your paperwork for release. I will have the nurse bring them to you when they are complete, along with your recovery instructions and the list of things to watch for. Take care, Mr. Bradley."

He strolls back out of the room, closing the curtain again as he leaves.

I am feeling a bit overwhelmed.

Two weeks?

How am I supposed to avoid an erection for two

whole weeks?

I am a healthy male in his prime, and I am practically a walking hard-on. I will never last two weeks without...wood.

Yet if I don't, they are going to cut my penis.

This is going to be the longest two weeks of my life.

Chapter Four

After finally arriving home, I manage to crawl into bed and get some sleep. We had stopped on the way for some Ibuprofen and an ice pack. I had taken two of the pills, and yes, it took the edge off.

The ice pack is sitting in the freezer, waiting for me this morning. Dante didn't end up coming to the hospital, as I was released before he was able to make it. He did send me a text however, letting me know that if I need anything, he will make himself available. I appreciate the sentiment, honestly, but I just want to be left alone to wallow in my misery. It is only a matter of time before the jokes start, and I would rather avoid that for now.

I gingerly roll out of bed, and I am surprised to find that the pain is minimal.

Thank God!

I am now standing beside the bed, and I know that I have to look, but I am afraid to. I also notice that there is a definite lack of morning wood. I am reassuring myself that this is part of the trauma that my poor penis has sustained, but I am starting to feel slightly panicked. The doctor didn't say anything about this! I seem to remember him telling me that morning woodies were something that I couldn't control.

Does that mean something is broken?

Oh God, no! No!

Alright, I am going to have to look. I manage to put on a pair of loose boxers before going to bed, so I will just have a peek inside and see what is going on. I pull the elastic waist of the boxers away from my body, take a deep breath, and look down.

At first, I don't believe what I am really seeing.

My penis looks like a bloated sausage!

It is sporting a grotesque shade of purple around the middle and along the right side, and the skin is so stretched in that area that there is a shine to it. I blink repeatedly, hoping that my eyes will see a different scene after they focus better.

Nope, that makes it even worse.

Now my vision is clearer, I'm noticing it looks even more horrific than it did upon my first inspection. I can see several, angry, raised veins, and it also appears that it looks slightly bent towards the left. I have to blink my eyes for a different reason now, as they are tearing up.

My beautiful penis is gone, and in its place is something out of a nightmare!

How am I supposed to recover from something like this?

I start to panic anew as I now feel the urge to go to the bathroom.

God, help me!

I will spare you the details, but I will say that although I was relieved to discover that there was almost no pain, it was not a pleasant experience. I didn't know how to handle it, literally. I rested my penis on my hand, instead of holding *The Big Guy*, and carefully aimed myself towards the toilet.

I won't say any more.

I trudge my way slowly towards the kitchen to get the ice pack and some more Ibuprofen. Once I have swallowed the pills with some water, I grab the ice pack and start the coffee.

I am thinking I might need something stronger than coffee this morning.

I gingerly place the ice pack against my former dick. Oh, that actually feels better. I have to remember to only keep it on for ten minutes.

I reach into the cupboard, grab a coffee mug and place it on the counter. I fill my cup and then hobble into the living room, with the ice pack at my crotch and my coffee mug.

After I am situated on the couch, I reach for my cell phone which has been charging on the end table. I check the screen to find that I have several missed texts. I open the message app to see that they are mostly from Logan. There is one from Dante and a few from others. I quickly read Dante's message and it is just a reminder to call if I need anything. I scan quickly through the others. Two are from women looking for a hook-up, one is from an investor that I have been in contact with for the club, and one is from a number that I don't recognize. I read that one next.

> **Hi Alex. I am sorry about your accident. I hope that you are feeling better soon. I am looking forward to working with you. If there is anything that I can do to help, please let me know. You can reach me at this number. Shayla**

OMG!

How the hell did she find out so soon, and who gave her my number? She is the last person I wanted knowing about this! I still have a small kernel of hope that I will heal on my own, that my dick will go back to being its glorious self, and I'll be able to seduce Shay, regardless of Logan's cock-blocking. How am I supposed to do that if she knows about "The Incident?"

I quickly save her number into my contacts, and then begin to read Logan's texts. Here is where my Judas is revealed. He explains that Shayla was asleep on his couch when he got home last night. Apparently she has a key to his place, and was waiting to discuss the details with him about her new job. He says that he only told her that he had been at the hospital with me due to a minor personal injury, and that I would be fine. Well, at least he didn't give her details.

Still, how do I avoid giving anything away? I am walking funny, need to take it easy, and avoid anything physical. She is going to notice and have questions. She works for a magazine which means that she is good at sniffing out a story. Well, she can just keep her sniffer away from my crotch!

Okay, that didn't sound right, but you get my meaning.

I need to send a text off to Logan, reminding him that I know all his secrets and asking him to keep my injury just that, a secret, unless he wants a few of his to surface around the club. I think he will keep this to himself. I am not worried about Dante as much, but I will ask him to keep this to himself as well.

I have just finished with my texts and coffee when there is a knock at my door.

I live in a very secure penthouse in a building that has its own security guard in the lobby. His name is Bert, and he is retired from the Army. He is very good at his job so I know that whomever is at the door has been through Bert first.

I put the ice pack aside. It has, after all, been ten minutes by now. I rise carefully from the couch to answer the door. I don't bother asking who it is, I just unlock and open it. Dante and Logan are standing on the other side. I should have known. I step aside for them to enter, shut the door, and we all head into the living room. Once we are all seated, I know "The Inquisition" is about to commence. I don't have to wait long. Dante cuts right to the chase.

"How bad is it?" His face gives nothing away. I have to assume that it is a genuine question and not the lead into a joke. Still, the less I reveal the better.

"Not too bad. Some discomfort, and there is some bruising and swelling. I should be fine to work. "

There, that doesn't sound too bad.

"Bullshit! I saw the way that you were walking, and Logan has given me the details from your time at the hospital." He is glaring at me now.

I turn and glare at Logan, who doesn't look at all bothered by his loose lips. I take a deep breath and try to sound as calm as possible.

"I am fine, really. Yes, it is uncomfortable, and yes, it isn't pretty in my pants. I am not going to let this problem interfere with my life however, any more than it already has. I am going to do all that the doctor instructed me to do and hope that everything goes back to normal in the time frame that I was given. There is nothing else to discuss here."

Logan and Dante share a look. I don't like the look. Logan doesn't shock me with what comes out of his mouth.

"Listen, we are all guys here. We know how close a guy is to his cock, and we just want to know how you are doing. With that being said, I didn't want to ask you last night, but I will now. How the hell did this happen?"

I am not going to give them a blow-by-blow of the events. I can't fault them for being curious, I would be too if this had happened to someone other than myself. Might as well get this out of the way.

"She was riding me, and somehow we shifted the angle. When she came back down, she bent my dick."

Both my friends are now staring at me in horror. Yep, it was horrific. Dante is the first to recover.

I can see the struggle on his face, as he decides what to say.

"I don't want the details, but how bent are we talking here?"

"Almost in half. There was a popping sound, and that is all I remember. The rest is a haze of pain."

The looks of horror are still on their faces, but now they are starting to look a little green.

I just realized that I never asked about what happened to Kylie, The Boner Bender, so I ask now. Apparently Dante was stuck with the task of taking care of her, as Logan came with me to the hospital. Dante assures me that he made sure that she was calm when she left, and was sent home in a cab that we paid for. She asked that she be informed on how I am doing. Dante took her cell phone number down, and has since sent her a text letting her know that I am home from the hospital and should be fine.

After discussing Kylie, The Manhood Mangler, the guys seem to be gearing up to something. I am getting a bad feeling here. Logan is trying to keep a straight face, but I know him, and he is failing. Here it comes.

"Can we see it?" Logan is trying not to snicker at this point.

Dante is nodding his head too.

Are you kidding me here?

I am not waving my sausage at them for their viewing pleasure!

I jump up from the couch in my anger, and I really shouldn't have done that for two reasons. One, the sudden movement jostles my dick around and I have to bite back a moan of pain. Two, still being in my boxers, I have now presented myself to the scrutiny of my friends. There is no hiding the evidence of my swelling now. Through the boxers, I am definitely showing a different form than usual. Being guys, we have all seen each other in our skivvies, or hell even naked. I am not bragging, okay maybe a little, but I usually fill out my underwear nicely. At the present moment, I am filling them to capacity.

I chance a look at my friends.

Their mouths are hanging open. I want to crawl into a hole at this point. Nothing is going to stop them now until they see *The Full Monty*.

"Alright, I will let you look, but just keep in mind that it looks worse that it feels," I say, waiting for a rousing chorus of "liar, liar, pants on fire" from one of them. "And there will be no touching!"

"Dude, seriously? No offense, but there will never be an occasion where I feel the need to touch your junk!"

I give Dante a nod, acknowledging that I heard him.

Logan is smirking. The bastard.

Without anything else to be said, I drop my boxers.

The silence speaks for itself. I am looking down at my package, hoping it isn't as bad as I remember now that I have iced it. Although, I think that the swelling looks a bit better, not much has changed.

I chance a look up at the guys. They have stepped closer, probably for a better look.

Shoot me now. I can feel my face burning with humiliation.

Wait for it.

Any minute now.

"Holy fuck!" This is Dante's reaction.

"I think that I am going to be sick." Logan is looking greener as he speaks.

I pull my boxers back up, done with this freak show. I continue to reassure them that it looks worse than it is, and after another round of remarks, they reluctantly agree to let me work tonight.

As if they could stop me!

I escort them to the door, promising to call if I need anything. Honestly, it is getting tiresome now. I tell them that I will see them tonight and gently shut the door. I stand with my forehead pressed against the back of it, and exhale with relief.

Tonight will have to be an Oscar-winning performance to reassure them that I can handle working in this condition and hide the evidence of my injury from everyone else.

Chapter Five

I manage to arrive at the club without anyone noticing.

I slip into the office to see if Logan has arrived yet. The office is empty, but it appears that he has been in here because his cologne is still lingering. Logan wears a very expensive cologne that the women seem to love. I personally prefer to wear something much less overpowering. I take a look at the monitors to see if I can spot him somewhere in the club. I see Dante making his security checks, but there is no sign of Logan. I scan every monitor, and I am just about to go out and look for him, when I see them.

He is walking out of one of the control rooms with Shay. I whimper at what my vision beholds. She has her hair up in some messy knot that woman do revealing her graceful neck. She is wearing one of the toga-style dresses that match this week's theme, and heaven help me, her body is lust-inspiring in it. Her curves are even more apparent in this dress than what she was wearing yesterday.

I am so enraptured by the goddess before me that I don't notice it at first. It is just a slight stirring, but my dick is definitely stirring! I almost want to weep with relief. This is the first sign of life that I have had from *The Big Guy*. I was starting to fear that Kylie, The Penis Popper, had killed him.

I know you might think that I am being melodramatic, but you have to understand how important our penises are to us. This was no minor catastrophe for me, but one of biblical proportions. I would rather lose the use of one of my limbs, or one of my senses, than the use of my favorite body part! Now that we have established that, I will continue.

They are heading to the bar area. I see Logan introducing her to some of the bar staff. The women are all smiling and shaking her hand while the men are all wearing shit-eating grins and nodding to her, shoving their hands in their pockets to adjust everything that has expanded. I feel for those guys. That is the same reaction that I had. Our head bartender, Mark, is taking his ogling to an indecent level, though. I don't think that he has made eye contact with her once, and she is speaking to him. I am just about to storm out there, when I see Logan get up in Mark's face. I don't have to hear what he is saying because Mark's face and body language says it all. Logan has just issued another cock-block. They are leaving the bar and it looks like they are heading here. I quickly move towards the desk, pick up the first paper I see, and pretend to be reading it. I don't need them knowing that I have been peeping at them. I see that it is Shay's application. I start to quickly scan, and memorize, all of her information. I am just about finished when they walk through the door.

"Alex! I didn't expect to see you tonight." Shay turns and looks to Logan after she says this.

Good, she won't see the daggers I am throwing at him. How bad did he make my "accident" sound?

"Alex is fine, Shay. I told you that it was a minor injury." He still won't look at me though.

Judas!

"No, you said that he hurt himself exercising, and damaged a muscle that needed to be seen by a doctor. I know how bad a muscle injury can be. You also didn't say which muscle, so I was assuming his arm or leg, in which case he would be off for a while."

I have to give Logan some credit for that. I suppose sex is a form of exercise, and it was my "love muscle" that was injured. Still, I know that she is going to ask where I am hurt. Might as well handle this now.

"I tore something in my leg." Yeah, the middle one. "And I have to take it easy, but otherwise I am good."

This will also, hopefully, explain the way that I am walking. I am actually feeling pretty good about my explanation, until she speaks again.

"Do you need help exercising and strengthening it? I could maybe massage the area for you, or help you with stretching it out."

At this, Logan turns around, but I can see his shoulders shaking.

I think my eyes have crossed at the thought of Shay doing all that she has just described to my "muscle." I also think that my dick heard her too, as there is some "stretching" trying to happen in my pants. I am mentally praising The Big Guy for his efforts.

Shay is looking at me hopefully now, and God help me, I am feeling hopeful as well, but for different reasons. I am hopeful that these stirrings in my loins mean that I am healing. And I am also hopeful that Shay will be able to demonstrate these techniques on me when I am recovered.

I know that I have to say something, but am at a loss as to what. Logan has recovered and saves me from answering her.

"I am sure that Alex appreciates your offer, Shay. He is a big boy, and I think that he can manage on his own. Besides, you have a job to begin tonight. On that note, I think that you are ready. You know where everything is, you have met some of the staff, we have been over the operations and procedures, and you have your schedule for the next few weeks. Were there any other questions that you had before your shift starts?"

Nice deflection, Logan!

"Actually, I do. Do I acknowledge our relationship should it come to light? Also, do I address you in the same manner as your staff?"

"I am not asking you to hide or deny our relationship. I just want to make sure that you are treated fairly. I don't want the staff to think that you are different than them, and they will if they find out that you are my cousin. They will imagine that you are getting preferential treatment over them and all sorts of other bullshit. This is also why we have the no dating policy, that way everyone remains equal. If it does come out, don't deny it as that will make it worse, but downplay how close we really are. If and when it happens, I guess we will deal with it then. For the same reason, it would be best that you address us all by our given names, the same as the staff. That would be Mr. Crawford for me, and Mr. Bradley and Mr. Valdez for Alex and Dante."

She nods to acknowledge this.

With nothing left to discuss, she excuses herself and says that she will see us on the floor. She shuts the door behind her and I slump against the desk. My first crisis has been averted. I look up to see that Logan is bent over, silently laughing his ass off. I find myself chuckling with him. Before I know it, we are both gasping and wheezing from laughing so hard.

This is when Dante decides to walk in. He closes the door and looks at both of us. His eyebrows are slowly climbing towards his hairline and a small smile is forming on his lips.

"Dare I ask what I missed?"

Logan recovers first. "Oh, just Shay offering to stretch and massage the 'muscle' that Alex has injured."

He uses air quotes and eyebrow bobs on the word "muscle," to get the message to Dante. Not one to miss a beat, Dante starts snickering.

"Dude, what makes her think he has an injured muscle that needs some personal therapy?"

"Logan hadn't given her any details about our trip to the hospital, thank you for that Logan, just that I had a minor injury. She wanted to know about the injury, so he gave her a very loose explanation about..." I use air quotes here. "...'tearing a muscle during exercise.' She then wanted to know where it was, so I told her my leg. I just didn't say it was the middle one."

Dante had been laughing harder through the air quotes, but by the end, he loses it completely. We are having a good laugh, when I realize that this is all at my expense. Suddenly, it isn't so funny anymore. The guys notice that I am not laughing, and try to control themselves.

"Ok, I have given a tour, and all the instructions that I could think of to Shay. She is on the floor now, getting ready to start her first shift. I know that I have said no special treatment, but she is family, and we look out for family. I also know that she wants to get the full experience here for her magazine, but I would feel better if we kept an eye on her. I have a ton of numbers to crunch." At this his face lights up. He is such a geek. "So Alex, can you keep an eye on her? Just try to look casual so that she, or anyone else, doesn't notice."

I perk up at this. I can do stealth.

Just call me, Bond!

"That's a good idea. I will be busy with security, and having Alex shadow her will give him something to do since he can't perform his usual duties."

"Hey, I am not disabled, and I'm right here! I know that I have to limit my duties, but I am not useless. I don't mind watching Shay, but don't act like you're doing me some favor here."

"Wow, someone forgot to take his Midol today! Relax man, that wasn't a stab at you. I was just pointing out that this will all work out, due to the circumstances."

"Circumstances? What would those be? I am sorry if my crippled cock has created 'circumstances' for you, Dante."

You could hear a pin drop after my little tantrum.

What's wrong with me now?

I thought it was the little head that got injured, not the big one. I hang my head, and let out the breath that I didn't even realize I had been holding.

"Jesus Alex, I'm sorry. I wasn't implying anything, just stating the facts. I didn't realize you were so sensitive about it."

I feel even worse now. He shouldn't be the one apologizing, it should be me.

Before I can do just that, Logan jumps in.

"Okay girls, let's put our manginas aside for now. Can we just focus on what needs to be done tonight, and leave it at that?"

"Fine, but I need to apologize first. I'm sorry, Dante. I shouldn't have snapped at you. I guess it really is bothering me more than I realized."

"No worries, my man. I know it would bother me too. I can't even imagine what you are going through. If my dick looked like something the dog dragged in, I would be sensitive too."

I just raise an eyebrow at him.

Really, that visual wasn't necessary, but apparently that was kind compared to what Logan has to add.

"Agreed. When I saw you at the hospital, I thought that was bad enough, but what you showed us today ranks on my top three list of most disgusting things that I have ever seen. One was Professor Miller's body when she decided to seduce me. If her old, wrinkly skin could flap she would have been able to fly! The worst though was my sister's cat after it had been filleted by the fan in my dad's car, where it had decided was the perfect place for a cat nap. There was fur and cat parts everywhere! Our garage looked like the scene of a massacre. Lissa never forgave Dad for that, although how he was supposed to know the stupid cat was in there is beyond me."

I scowl at Logan.

How does he expect me to feel after my penis has been compared to kitty mulch and wrinkled skin flaps?

We have heard these particular horror stories before so there was nothing new there, but to be compared to them? My dignity can only handle so much and I am getting worked up again.

Dante seems to realize that I am at the end of my rope and he comes over to pat me on the back.

"Seriously Alex, we don't envy what you are going through, and we will try to be more sensitive. Come on, I will walk you out."

I don't even bother saying anything. I just trot myself behind him and out the door, with my penis that resembles a saggy, minced, cat part that the dog dragged in.

Chapter Six

After I slink away from Dante so that I can lick my wounds a bit, I decide to begin my spy mission.

It is easy to spot Shay. I just have to follow the drool puddles on the floor to the crowd of men who are surrounding her. She is serving a table of what looks like college kids. The guys at the table are chatting her up while a small hoard of men are hovering close to the edge, trying to look like they are just casually standing around.

I mentally roll my eyes at this.

Picking up my pace, I stride over to a table that is two down from her. I proceed to politely ask the people at the table if they are enjoying themselves while keeping an eye on Shay. The two young couples at the table ensure me that they are indeed having a good time, and commend me on the concept of the club. I thank them, and continue my circuit of the tables near Shay.

She has finally managed to free herself from her fans and is at the bar, getting drink orders for another table. The men at the bar are all turned slightly towards her, trying to sneak peeks without being too obvious.

I'm starting to agree with Logan about not wanting her to work here.

Our girls are all beautiful in their own right, and garner plenty of attention, but this is ridiculous. I don't know how she is able to ignore all of the eye-humping going on.

She turns fluently around, with her tray in her hands, and sashays back to her section.

I am so entranced by her that I don't notice the other show that has commenced. Over at the back corner by the hall leading to the security and computer rooms, it appears that Logan and Laney are having a heated discussion. Logan is gesturing with his hands, while Laney's whole body is gesturing, and it is saying, "Back Off!" But Logan seems to be ignoring the message. I am about to head that way to see if they need a timeout, when Laney turns abruptly, and storms off.

What was that all about?

Usually, Logan is flirting with her while she ignores him. They banter back and forth a lot, but it is always friendly.

Logan hangs his head, and appears to be taking deep breaths.

I have seen enough and walk over to my friend. When I approach, Logan lifts his head and looks at me. I can't decipher the look, but it is not a good look.

"What happened, Logan? I just saw you and Laney having what appeared to be some kind of argument?"

"I was asking her if she could keep an eye on our 'new' girl tonight and make sure that she is okay. I don't know how, but she took my concern for Shay as interest. She recited back to me all my reasons for the no-dating policy with the staff, and then called me a few choice words. I was trying to explain to her that I was just concerned about our newest staff member, when she suddenly turned around and stomped off. I don't understand her."

He might not understand her, but I think that I do.

Jealousy is an ugly bitch.

This is something that I didn't see coming. I thought Laney was immune to Logan, but apparently something has changed, or she just hid it well.

Oh, the fun I can have with this!

I don't want to alert Logan to my musings, so I quickly steer the topic back to Shay.

"I am sure that she will be back to playing nice with you by tomorrow. In the meantime, I am a little concerned myself about Shay. She seems to be drawing a lot of unsavory attention. As the alcohol starts to really hit some of these guys, it could escalate."

"I was afraid of this. It was one of the reasons that I didn't want her to work here. She has developed into a stunning woman. When she and Lissa are anywhere together, I nearly have a heart attack. I fear for them constantly."

Logan's sister Lissa, short for Elisabeth, is a real-life Barbie doll. She has the long blonde hair, the big blue eyes, and is tall and tanned with an eye-popping set of breasts. Logan has been protecting her since they were kids. Where Shay has grown into her looks, Lissa has always been beautiful. Dante and I are also very protective of her. She is a sister to all of us.

"Alex, is there some way that you can arrange for her to work a certain section and then instruct Dante to only send women to that section?" He has an almost desperate look on his face now.

I am feeling a little desperate myself.

"I can ask Dante if he can send the female flow to a certain section, but we can't control where they sit. Women like to be close to the dance floor, so maybe we can try putting a few tables together for bigger groups and having a reserved sign on them. Then when a group of women come in, Dante can let them know that those tables are available for them. What do you think?"

"I think, that you are a genius! She will still have to serve other tables until those are filled and go the bar for orders, but it should cut her interactions with the men in half. Brilliant! See if you can talk to Dante about it while I go and make the arrangements for the tables."

Logan hurries away, and I head for the security check at the door where Dante will be.

I find Dante leaning against a wall, keeping a close watch on the crowd by the door. Two of our beefiest security guys are checking I.D.'s, while two more are controlling the line outside the door. Dante turns to me at my approach, and I must look like I am on a mission because Dante straightens and faces me full-on.

"Logan and I have come up with a plan to curb some of the unwanted male attention surrounding Shay. We are going to put some of the tables together for larger groups, and she will be assigned there. Can you encourage groups of women to head for those tables? We are going to put a reserved card on the tables so they remain free."

"I can certainly try. How large of a group are we talking here?"

"Good question. If we put two tables together, those would hold groups of eight to ten comfortably on the lounges."

"Alright, I will see what I can do here. You do realize that if she finds out why you are doing this to her, she'll be wearing your balls as earrings, right?"

I'm sure she will, right after she takes Logan's.

"She doesn't need to know anything about it. All the wait staff are assigned a section."

"If you say so, my man. I'll text you when there appears to be a group of women, but they sometimes have a few guys with them."

"A few guys are fine, just do what you can. I'm going to find Logan and see how he is making out with the tables."

Dante smirks. "It was nice knowing you guys."

I flip him the bird, and head back inside the club to seek out Logan.

I don't have to look too hard. He doesn't usually venture into the club when we are open for a reason. There is a mass of eager bodies surrounding him. He is politely trying to evade the women, but some are very persistent, and I think that I just saw one grab his ass! Time to help him out. I wade into the sea of women and draw some of the attention my way. He shoots me a grateful look. We are dodging hands, and accepting a few numbers to speed things up, when I feel heat on the back of my neck.

Logan must feel it too, because we turn behind us in unison. Shay and Laney are glaring at us. Shay has her tray perched perfectly on her shoulder, held by her beautiful, dainty hands. Laney doesn't have a tray at the moment, so her hands are on her hips, and one of her feet is tapping out an angry beat against the floor.

Logan manages to break away from the women first, and rushes over to Shay. He leans down and whispers something into her ear. Her face loses some of its anger, and she nods her head. She then turns to the bar and asks one of the other waitresses if she can deliver her drinks to her tables. She follows Logan down the hall behind the bar, presumably to the office.

I look at Laney, and for a brief moment, I think I see something that looks like longing on her face, but it is gone too fast for me to be sure.

"I hope she knows what she is getting with him. He is like a perfect cut of meat; heavenly to eat, and worth savoring every bite, but not what you get every day."

With these parting words of wisdom, she walks away.

I am dying inside at Logan being compared to a piece of meat!

I guess that I better head back to the office, incase Logan needs me to help him re-attach his balls. I am relieved, when walking down the hall, that I don't hear any yelling coming from the office. I knock on the door, and ease it open. Logan is at his desk, and Shay is perched on the corner. There is silence as I enter the room. They both look towards me, as I make my way in. Logan is looking at me when he begins to speak, and I can easily see that he is trying to make a point here.

"I was just explaining to Shay, that she would be able to gain more information for her article if she were in a more central location. I also explained to her that we are giving her two large tables instead of four or five smaller ones, because she is new and there would be less trips to the bar." He is staring hard at me now, and I know he wants me to agree with him, and follow his lead.

I have to give him credit, that all sounds very logical.

"I agree with Logan. Also, this will give you more time to gather information and observe what happens around you." I hope that sounds plausible to her.

Shay nods her head, but doesn't say anything.

Logan is shooting me pleading glances.

What else am I supposed to say?

I rack my brain to come up with something else, when I think of something. "Shay, how else can we help you get the information that you require?"

That sounds good, right?

"So you really are trying to help me, and you're not doing this because you don't have any faith in my abilities?" She looks at us both with wounded, puppy dog eyes.

Jesus, I never thought she would think that!

Obviously neither did Logan, by the look of horror on his face.

"Never did we think that, Shay. I saw how hard you were working out there. You made it look like you have been doing this for years, not just one night. We are only looking out for you." Logan looks panicked.

"What happened to treating me the same as the others?"

"I know that I said that, and yes we will be treating you the same as everyone else in public, but you are family, and I just want to make this easier for you." Logan stands from behind his desk, and pulls her into a hug. "Please let me do this for you. I will talk with the staff and explain that we are doing this because you are new. We haven't hired anyone for a while, so I can say that this is a strategy that we are implementing for our new employees. I can be pretty convincing, so don't worry about the others."

I am bouncing from foot-to-foot, hoping that I will get a chance to hug-it-out with her too. My dick is starting to twitch at the thought, which is really starting to give me hope for The Big Guy's recovery. Logan lets Shay go, and looks into her eyes. Whatever he sees there, makes him smile.

I am smiling now too, but for a different reason. As visions of being surrounded by all Shay's womanly softness have been playing out in my mind, my dick has turned the twitch into a mini-erection!

"Okay, Logan, I will accept your help. But if it becomes an issue, I will go back to waiting the regular tables. I really don't mind."

She might not, but we do.

Logan agrees, reluctantly. His look towards me screams, "Make it work!" Failure is not an option.

I do not want to watch Shay be visually molested every night that we are open. I am the only one who should be doing that.

Shay slides off her perch on the desk, and comes around to stand before me. I am holding my breath, waiting to see what she will do. She gives me a shy smile, and reaches her slender arms up to encircle my neck. I gingerly return the hug while keeping my lower body from direct contact. I don't want to risk a full-on erection and hurting myself. She feels like heaven in my arms. She is the perfect height for me, coming just under my nose, which is at the moment releasing the breath that I was holding and inhaling the scent of her hair. I don't dare look up at Logan. I can feel his eyes burning me. She eases back and I let her go. My dick lets out a tiny sigh, and relaxes in my pants once again. She thanks me for my help as well, and then glides past me and out the door.

I am still staring at the door and refusing to look at Logan. I know my verbal smack down is coming any minute now. I don't have to wait long.

"What the fuck was that, Alex? I told you that she is off limits yet you practically humped her leg!"

"I barely touched her and you know it! I am not exactly up to anything more than that right now, or did you forget about my broken dick?"

"No, I didn't forget, but it won't be broken forever. I see the way that you look at her when you think that I'm not looking, but you can forget it. She is family!"

"Hmmm ... just like Laney is an employee, and we don't touch the employees, right?"

"What the hell does that have to do with anything? I have never touched Laney."

"Yet, but we all see the way you chase her. It is only a matter of time."

"I can have any woman that I want. I don't chase women."

"Yes, you do. And it's because she doesn't fall at your feet, like all the others."

"She is an employee and nothing more. Sure, I flirt with her, but that is as far as it will go. This isn't about me and Laney though, this is about Shay and what is best for her."

"She is a grown woman and can make her own decisions. I will respect your wishes for now since I am in no condition to launch a seduction, but you cannot dictate my life any more than you can hers."

Logan sighs, and runs his hands through his hair. "Look Alex, Shayla is young and naive. She still believes in love and fairytale endings. She hasn't been hurt enough to become jaded about love, like us. I want her to find her prince and have her fairytale, just like I want the same for Lissa. We don't do love, we do sex. We are not the prince in the fairytale that swoops in and saves the day, we are the villains who break their hearts."

Wow, that has given me some serious insight into Logan. I have never said that I don't believe in love, or that I don't want it. Apparently, Logan has some issues with love. I wonder what happened to him in his past to make him feel this way.

Anyway, time to correct him about me.

"Logan, I do believe in love, and want that for myself someday. Sure, I enjoy the pleasures that I can find with a woman, and have enjoyed them plenty. But, if I meet the right one, no other woman would matter to me. I haven't gone looking for love, but I want it. I am not saying that Shay is the woman for me, but shouldn't we be given the opportunity to find out? I will promise to respect her, and I would never hurt her. I understand that you don't want her hurt, but I would not lead her on, or promise her something that I can't give her. I will not pursue her while she is working here, but I can't promise you that I won't try to get close to her. I am very attracted to her, and I think that it goes both ways."

"Yes, it goes both ways. She has basically said the same things to me. Alright, you are not to pursue her publicly, but what you do on your own time is your business. Just know that if you hurt her, what your junk looks like now, is nothing compared to how it will look when I get through with you."

I ignore the warning, because I have no intention of hurting her, and concentrate on the first part.

Shay feels the same way?

I'm starting to feel like a girl, sitting here talking about love with my friend, but this makes it all worthwhile.

I feel like fist-pumping the air!

After a few more threats to my genitals, Logan and I come to an understanding. I am so giddy at these turn of events that I practically float out of the office. I wouldn't have let him stop me from pursuing her, but it will make it easier with him lifting the cock-block.

Let the courting of Shayla Crawford begin!

Chapter Seven

The rest of the evening seems to go smoothly.

Shay works the two larger tables that we assign to her, and they are seated with mostly female patrons. For the most part, she isn't harassed. There are a few brave fellows, but they are quickly taken care of…by me. Shay doesn't seem to notice that I'm lurking, or at least she never indicates that she does. Logan and I pat ourselves on the back for a job well done at the end of the night.

I then trundle home, have a small drink of scotch, and head for bed.

It is important that you know that I have forgotten about my situation down under. I have taken my clothes off, down to my boxers, and then I climb into bed.

It is now morning, and I am groggily entering the conscious world. I roll over, and look at the clock, which reads 9:41am. I am usually up before ten on the nights that we are open, and before seven on the nights that we are closed.

Just in case you are wondering, we are open Thursdays through Saturdays. Thursdays are "Ladies Night," where there is no cover charge, normally five dollars, and they get a coupon for a free drink the next time they come. Fridays are "Boys Night Out," which is the same as Ladies Night, but for the men. Saturdays are our biggest nights. We advertise our theme for the week, encouraging people to dress for that destination, and give out prizes for the best dressed.

Today is Friday, which means I can't linger in bed, because there is always a lot to be done before we open.

I roll over onto my stomach to grab my phone off the other night stand where I have accidentally left it.

Big mistake!

I instantly roll back over, groaning and cupping myself.

Omigod, how did I forget about my poor penis?

I hadn't taken any pills last night when I got home for the swelling or the pain. I am breathing heavily and panting slightly. I don't want to look, I can feel how swollen it is. Wait a minute, this doesn't feel like the same swelling from yesterday. I gingerly feel the outline through my boxers.

Long, thick and hard.

I am feeling an erection!

I'm not broken, just bent!

I spring up out of bed, ignoring the pain. I quickly yank my boxers down and out of the way for a look. Well, my excitement drains quite a bit at what I am seeing.

Yes, I have a morning woody, but my dick is still slightly curved to the side, and is now a disgusting mix of purple, green and brown. If my penis was yellow, I would be looking at a bruised banana.

I reach down and start touching around the shaft, checking for tenderness.

The pain seems to be isolated to the right side, where the bend happened. I take a firm, yet gentle hold, and give an experimental stroke.

Don't judge me, it is for scientific purposes!

I am pleasantly surprised to find that, apart from the one area, it feels glorious! Oh, how I wish that I could continue with this, but I know that I have to stop, doctor's orders and all. I reluctantly release my dick, and I can practically hear him begging me to continue.

I know, Big Guy, me too.

After taking care of business in the bathroom, and grabbing a quick shower, I am dressed and in my kitchen making coffee. I chose my outfit carefully, with seduction in mind. I usually dress in casual, business attire on the nights that we are open, but tonight I am dressed to impress, in one of my designer suits. It is charcoal grey in color, and has been tailored to my measurements. I have paired this with a black silk dress shirt that shows off my chest nicely through the material. I hate ties, and only wear them for weddings, funerals, and business meetings. I usually just run some gel through my hair and let it dry on its own, but today I have spent some time stroking my ego in front of the mirror since I can't stroke other things. I have artfully styled my hair to give it that rumpled look that women seem to love. I am feeling pretty good about myself, despite my purple penis. I am keeping the faith where that is concerned, since anything else is not an option for me.

I grab my favorite mug, and pour my coffee. I look around my kitchen, imaging how Shay might see my apartment. In the kitchen, I have stainless steel appliances, granite counter tops, ceramic tile backsplash and floor, and an island in the center of the room with bar stools around it. I hand-picked everything that went into my condo, and I am proud of the finished results. The living room has a flat screen TV mounted on the wall above the fireplace and I have a sectional couch and two recliners that are grouped around a marble table. My bedroom has a California King bed, a nightstand on either side of the bed and two dressers across from it. I also have a huge walk-in closet. There is a guest room which I use as an office. I have a guest bathroom, and one off my bedroom. My bathroom has a walk-in shower with eight shower heads, and a Jacuzzi tub is recessed in the corner.

Nice!

The colors in my condo are all very neutral beiges, creams and browns. The only room with a different color is my bedroom. I opted for white walls, with navy blue trim. My bedspread is navy blue and white as well. This is the only room that is carpeted, which is plush and white. The furniture in this room is white-washed instead of brown to match the color scheme.

Masculine, yet elegant.

Okay, now I sound like a pussy.

I like nice things, and I have good taste, which my home reflects. I have worked hard to achieve my success, but I am not a snob. I keep my place spotless, and have a cleaning lady that comes by once a week just to give it a final polish.

Logan is worse than I am for extravagance with his home, and he is O.C.D. about having everything a certain way. I think it is because he grew-up poor, whereas Dante and I come from middle-class families. Dante is the most modest of our trio with his home. Just the bare necessities, and typical stuff you would find in a bachelor pad.

I finish my coffee and put the mug in the dishwasher. After grabbing my phone, keys and wallet, I am out the door.

I take the elevator down to the private garage. I have two vehicles, my reliable S.U.V, and my baby. My baby is a 2007 Porsche 911 GT2, in black.

I know that you are thinking this is a very pretentious car, but I am a guy, and we love our metal.

I am taking my baby out today, because I enjoy the ride and to impress a certain vixen. After stroking her a few times, I get inside my car. She is my favorite girl, and nothing can bring me down when I am with her. I start her up, and let her rev for a minute before I shift her into drive and head out of the garage. I reach into the console for my sunglasses and turn on the CD player. Demons, by Imagine Dragons is blaring out of my speakers, and I am on my way.

☺

When I arrive at the club, I notice that I am not the only one that wanted to get an early start today.

Dante's Harley Davidson, Night Rod is parked in his spot. I don't know how he can ride that thing, but he claims that the women love it, and so does he. I head inside to look for him, before going to the office.

The first thing that I notice is the lack of noise. It is usually pretty quiet during the day, but not like this. We have a tech crew that works during the day to ensure that the computers and programs are functioning properly and a cleaning crew that comes in and polishes the floors and sanitizes the bathrooms and the bar area. But today, there is no one around.

Where is everyone?

I hear the distant sound of voices coming from the back hallway that leads to our computer and security rooms, so I head in that direction. The voices are getting louder as I near the computer room, and there is definitely laughter now too. The door to the room is slightly ajar, so I am able to peek in without being noticed. There are four tech guys, Dante, and two of his security staff, all huddled around a computer. The laughter continues, as I ease into the room to take a closer look at the screen. I now see what all the commotion is about.

There, on the screen, is an image of a naked woman with anatomically impossible breasts. It really is rather amusing, and I find myself chuckling.

Dante and two of the other men hear me, and turn around.

"Hey man, how's it hanging?"

Dante manages to ask this with a straight face, the jerk! I decide to have a little fun with him as payback. He has a bottle of water in his hand, and is just about to take a drink.

"Oh you know, slightly swollen and a bit to the left," I smirk.

Dante starts to choke on the gulp of water he had just swallowed. The tech guys are in a panic, and move him away from the equipment, as he is coughing, and spluttering.

Revenge is sweet!

He finally gets control of himself, and walks over to me.

He slaps me on the back, hard.

"I deserved that. Glad to see that your sense of humor is back. Are you going to be around for a bit?"

"Yeah, I came in to get some paperwork done, and some numbers ready for Logan to jerk-off with."

Logan probably could use numbers for his spank bank. The guy has a serious hard-on for them.

"That guy needs to get laid more. Have you noticed that he hasn't been going home with anyone?"

"Maybe he has been hooking-up with women somewhere else?" As I ask this, I am already doubting it.

Logan has become quite uptight lately. He is more laid back when he is getting some. Come to think of it, I can't remember the last time he mentioned a sexcapade. I will admit to being the slut of the group, but the other two are not living like monks. I'll have to ask him about it.

"I don't think so. He has been practically living here, and staying in the apartment upstairs most nights."

"Alone, in the Love Nest?"

This is not sounding good.

"Yes, and frankly that makes me wonder what is really going on. Do you think it has anything to do with his obsession with Laney?"

Dante has hit the nail on the head with that question. I am almost positive that our lovely Laney is at the root of this development with Logan.

"Let me see what I can find out and I will let you know. Do you have any invoices that I need to go over for the computer programming or security?"

Dante and I head to his security office to collect the invoices that I need. I am heading to the office with these when I notice a person detach from the bar.

I don't recognize her at first because she is just wearing jeans and a t-shirt, but then I realize who I am staring at with perfect clarity, and a sense of horror.

Kylie is approaching me warily. I can only imagine what she sees on my face, and I feel bad, but can't help it. Logically, I know that "The Incident" was an accident, but there is nothing logical about my fear. My penis has let out a silent scream and retreated, and my mind is replaying a constant loop of the terrifying events. I am paralyzed, and can't form a single word. She must realize this, because she saves me from embarrassing myself by speaking first.

"Dante said it was okay to come by today. I just wanted to see how you were doing, and to tell you how sorry I am about, well, you know." Her eyes are full of honesty, and they are pleading with me to accept her apology.

I feel like a bastard for making her feel that she needs to apologize at all.

"Kylie, there is nothing for you to apologize for. It was an accident. I will be fine, honestly."

At this she looks hopeful. "Really? I know Dante told me that you were fine, but I didn't believe him. I had never heard a man scream so much from pain, and then passing out from it."

Well, that is truly mortifying.

Not the way a man wants to be remembered in the bedroom.

There is really nothing that I can say to this. I was screaming, and I did pass out. I can hear Pride packing his bag, and asking, Humility if he wants to join him.

How do I redeem myself after that?

"Kylie, yes it hurt very much at the time, and unless you are a man, you wouldn't understand how painful it was. But, I assure you that I am healing, and I will be fine."

At this, she chews her lip. I am dreading what might come out of her mouth.

My dread is validated.

"Out of curiosity, can I see it?" she quickly rushes on. "My friends didn't believe me when I told them about how it bent and the sound it made. They said that you were faking your injury, and that it isn't possible. I just want to know for myself, you know?"

Omigod!

She did *not* just ask to see it and tell me that she has told her friends!

Humility has left the building, and I am pretty sure that Ego is hot on his trail. I cannot believe that she is asking to see my dick after she broke it. I must be glaring at her now, for she backs up a bit.

Time for some damage control.

"I do not think that it is necessary for me to prove my injury to you. Also, I don't appreciate the fact that you are discussing my personal injury with your friends."

She starts to cry.

I panic, as I am not good around crying women.

I try patting her on the shoulder, but she decides that isn't enough, and launches herself at me. She is mumbling apologies, and basically snotting all over my expensive shirt. I try to pull away slightly, but she just clings harder.

So here I am, trying to comfort a distraught Kylie, when she tilts her head up, and latches her lips onto mine.

It is at this moment that Shay walks into the bar.

Chapter Eight

In a blind panic, I am trying to untangle myself from Kylie. She must take this as a sign of encouragement instead and lets out a moan, as she tries climbing me like a tree. I am staggering around, yanking at Kylie to let go. I dare not look at Shay, for this must look worse by the second. I finally manage to tear my lips away from Kylie and gasp out a command for her to stop. She freezes, and looks at me with absolute mortification.

I almost take pity on her...almost.

She took it upon herself to put us both is this awkward situation. She releases her hold on me and I immediately step back.

I chance a look in Shay's direction, but she is no longer there. I look back to Kylie, and her head is hanging. I have to rectify this.

"Kylie, I am sorry if I led you to believe that what you just did was reciprocated. I am not in any way looking to rekindle what we shared the other night. You are a very nice girl, and I wish you all the best, but we will not be seeing each other again." I try to say this as gently as possible, but I am not at all happy about what just happened. I now have to find Shay, and fix her assumptions of what she just saw, without giving away too much. Kylie just nods her head, and turns to leave, but at the last moment lifts her head high and stares me straight in the eye.

"I knew you had a reputation, but I had no idea just what a jerk you are. This is your loss, and I hope your dick is permanently damaged so that you can't do this to another woman!" With these hostile words spat at me, she spins on her heel and storms off.

Not the first time that a woman has taken rejection from me with a burst of indignation, but it is the first time that one has wished ill against my poor penis.

Hasn't he suffered enough?

Plus, I am the victim here! Ugh, I don't have time to worry about Kylie's hurt feelings, I have to find Shay.

I head in the direction of the office, but only manage to take a few steps before I spot her. She is sitting on one of the barstools, and she is looking directly at me. I approach slowly, not sure of the welcome I will receive. As I get closer, I notice that she looks more intrigued than upset. I would rather have her upset than curious. I have to ascertain how much of that she has heard.

"I am sorry that you had to witness that, Shay. It wasn't how it looked."

At this, she arches her eyebrow. "Really? Well, to me, it looked like a woman who knows you, and was hoping to continue knowing you, but you rejected her. Am I wrong?"

Nope, not wrong at all, dammit!

How am I going to explain this without revealing my injury, or looking bad? I know they say, "The truth will set you free," but I am not about to Free Willy!

"You are not wrong, but you don't have the complete story. Yes I know her, and yes she was a bit presumptuous about where things were going, but I could have been more forceful with her before she took it that far."

"Don't make excuses for her. From what I could tell, you were very clear with your message. I am sure you didn't encourage her. Some women just don't take rejection well."

"Wait a minute, are you defending me? You aren't mad?"

"Why would I be mad? It doesn't concern me. What does concern me though, is that she implied there is something wrong with you, besides a pulled muscle. Just what were you doing to hurt yourself...in more than one place?"

Omigod!

What am I supposed to say to that?

By the look on her face now, she has it figured out, without any explanations needed. Time to come clean.

Good-bye, to any chance that I might have had.

"There is just the one injury, and we were not lying, exactly, when we told you that it was a muscle, or that I was exercising. I was intimate with that woman you just saw. I injured a part of my body that is private, and I didn't want anyone knowing. I am sorry that we misled you."

By the time I get to the end of this, I am staring at the floor.

I can't bear to see the disgust that is surely on her face. There is silence around us, but I can hear my heart hammering in my chest. Any minute now she is going to tell me what she thinks of me, and run away as far and fast as she can. I can't blame her, for what woman wants to learn that her potential suitor isn't fully functional, and a liar on top of it.

I am just about to leave and slink away, when a slender hand comes into view, and rests over my arm. I look up, and into eyes filled with kindness, not condemnation.

"Alex, I already gathered that you must have been intimate with that woman, and that doesn't bother me. Yes, you deceived me about your injury, but I understand why. Do you really believe any of this would change my opinion of you, or matter to me?"

I am speechless.

I stand there like a moron with a lump in my throat. Yes, I did think it would change how she saw me, and matter to her. How can she sit there so calmly and completely undo me with her kind nature and generous heart? I clear my throat and finally find my voice.

"I'm sorry, but to any other woman, it would bother them."

"I am not any other woman, as you will find out. I am sorry that you were hurt, and even more so that you are letting it affect how you feel about yourself. You are more than your penis, Alex."

I burst out laughing. Probably a release from all the stress.

She joins me, and soon we are both laughing and smiling. God, could this woman be any more perfect?

After the laughter subsides, I notice I am feeling much better. I ask her if I can take her out on a date sometime next week, and she readily agrees. We make arrangements for Tuesday, when I will pick her up for lunch. She slides off her stool and tells me that she will see me later, as she has plenty to do today herself. She just stopped by to leave a message for Logan, since he isn't answering his phone.

This news has me a bit concerned.

I give her a gentle hug and agree to text her if I get a hold of Logan. I watch her leave, and then head straight to the stairs leading to the Love Nest.

Time to find out what is up with Logan.

I am imagining quite a few scenarios as to why Logan is holed-up in the apartment upstairs, but none of them are even close to the reality. I knock on the door, and when there is no answer, I turn the knob to find it unlocked. I ease the door open and peek inside. I see his keys on the hall table, so I am assured that he is here. I walk inside and shut the door behind me.

There is no sign of Logan, but there is evidence that he is here all around me. I am not sure what disturbs me more, the empty bottles lining the coffee table, or his clothes strewn about the furniture. Logan rarely drinks and he is a neat freak.

What happened here?

I hear a grunt from the bedroom, followed by a snore. Well, there is no mystery as to where Logan is anymore. I walk towards the bedroom to find the door is wide open. There, on the bed, is my friend.

Well, what once resembled my friend.

He is lying face-up, with his mouth agape, and small snores are escaping from him. He is in his boxer-briefs, thank God! I have seen him naked before, but that doesn't mean that I want to see him naked now. His hair is a disheveled mess, and his arms are above his head. The blankets are strewn all over the floor, and there is as definite odor of alcohol wafting from him.

Logan is passed-out drunk.

I'm debating if I should call Dante, when Logan begins to stir awake. He starts smacking his lips, brings his arms down to his face, and rubs his mouth. Yeah, I bet he is feeling like his tongue is sporting a sweater. He squints his eyes open a fraction, and lets out a groan. He hasn't realized that I am here yet. He is staring at the ceiling, and I decide to have some fun with him.

"Good morning, Sunshine!" I might have said this rather loudly.

Logan tries to shoot out of the bed, but his legs become tangled in the last sheet left on it, and he falls over the side. There is a thump, followed by groaning, and a few choice words. I am trying to silence my mirth, but I know that he hears me.

Oh, well.

"What the hell, Alex?"

"Just checking to make sure that you are alive, seeing as no one knew where you were, or how you were doing."

"I didn't realize that I have to answer to anyone now."

"Well, we were just getting a bit concerned, and rightfully so by the looks of it. What happened to you?"

"Nothing happened. Can't I have a few drinks without, The Inquisition?"

"Sure, if it was just a few drinks and not the whole bar! Do you even know how much you drank?"

I am pretty sure he mumbles, "Not nearly enough", but what he says is, "Not that much."

"Logan, I counted at least eight bottles of beer, and there were a few liquor bottles opened out there too."

He gets up from the floor, and grabs onto the bed to steady himself. He is in pretty rough shape. He doesn't bother answering me, just staggers past me and down the hall to the bathroom.

I decide to head out to the living room, and start cleaning up.

After I have gathered the bottles and the clothes, I head into the kitchen to start some coffee. I was going to dump the liquor bottles, but change my mind as Logan might need some hair of the dog. I just finish pouring the coffee for us when, The Walking Dead enters the kitchen. He has managed to put his pants on, but that's as far as he has gotten. He looks like shit, with bags under his blood-shot eyes, and his hair still sticking up in all directions.

"Thanks for tidying-up. Is that coffee?" His eyes brighten a bit at the sight of the liquid gold.

"Yes, and I am going to put a little something in it to help you with your hangover."

"Just a little. I don't think I can handle anymore."

"Are you going to tell me what happened now, that sent you into an alcoholic binge?"

"Nope." He grabs the coffee that I have doctored for him, and heads back into the living room. I have no choice but to follow, especially if I want answers.

He sits in one of the chairs, hugging his mug with both hands, and sipping slowly. I sigh, and head over to the couch across from him. I just sit there and stare at him, hoping he will cave and just tell me. He doesn't. He is studiously ignoring me. I decide to get his attention.

"I asked Shay out for lunch on Tuesday, and she accepted. Of course, this was right after she saw me with Kylie trying to suck my lips off, and ride me like a stripper pole."

He spews the mouthful of coffee he had taken. He wipes his mouth, and looks at me finally.

"How did that happen? I figured she was the last woman on earth you would let near you again."

True, but I am just baiting him with this, so I will not be answering that until he spills. "I don't feel like talking about it."

Logan scowls at me. He is catching on now. He lets out a grunt, and drops his head back against the chair. "You are worse than a woman. Okay, the truth is that I tried talking to Laney last night before she left. It didn't go well. Actually, that is an understatement. She accused me of some horrible things, including seducing Shayla. She wouldn't even give me the chance to explain. The worst part is though, after her verbal assault on me, she quit."

Okay, I didn't see that coming!

Laney quit?

Now I can see how this would cause Logan to spiral out of control last night. He will never admit it, but I suspect that he has developed feelings for her and doesn't know how to handle them. Hence, he's acting like an ass around her and obsessing over her. Losing your favorite toy will bring any boy to his knees.

I am going to have to talk to Dante about this.

Looks like we have to grab a bull by the horns and this is going to be more than a one man job.

Chapter Nine

I have a little chat with Dante about what I had discovered in The Nest. We both agree that Laney needs to be contacted and set straight about Shay, but Logan is the main focus.

Dante manages to coax him back to the land of the living. Logan swears he's never drinking like that again, and I believe him. Dante offers to drive him home, so he can change his clothes.

I head down to the office and settle some paperwork, and go over all the details for the night. I also call Laney and leave a message for her to call me back, explaining that I don't normally put myself in the middle of a problem, but she needs to hear the truth. I sure hope that she calls back, otherwise I'm not sure what else to do. We have addresses for all the employees, but I'm not comfortable with the thought of tracking her down at home. That just screams of desperation.

I'm just finishing up on the computer, when my cell phone rings. I chance a look at the screen before answering, and am relieved to see Laney's number.

"Laney, I am so glad that you called."

"I almost didn't, but I have always liked you, Alex. I know you wouldn't be butting in unless it mattered to you."

"You're right, it does matter to me. I will be straight with you Laney, and tell you the truth. Shayla is Logan's cousin. We didn't want anyone knowing, just in case they treated her differently. I am sure you can imagine how some of the staff would react if they knew."

There's a heavy silence on the other end of the phone. I almost thought for a minute that she hung up, but she finally says, "I believe you, and that also explains her perfect looks. Damn, what a gene pool they have in that family. I have to say that I am a little hurt though. I thought that I was more than just an employee, and that I had proven myself to be trustworthy. If you wanted me working so closely with her, you should have just been honest with me. I would have understood and kept it to myself, but it doesn't really matter anymore, since I quit last night."

"You are still an employee here. No one wants to see you leave, and you would have to give us more notice than that anyways. You are an excellent staff member, but trust me, you are more than that to us as well. I am sorry that you feel hurt, that wasn't our intention. The whole situation with Shay happened so fast, and we have been working on the fly with what we have."

"You still want me to work for you? What about Dante and…Logan?"

"Of course I do, and so do the others. Especially Logan, since he feels responsible for your quitting in the first place."

"I will have to apologize to him, but not too soon. Gotta make him sweat a bit." She laughs at this, and I feel a huge weight lift from my shoulders.

Tragedy avoided.

Yes!

"Sure hun, make him suffer a little, we all enjoy watching him squirm."

"Thanks, Alex. Regardless what women say about you guys, I know you are all decent men. I honestly don't know what got into me."

I do, and it is not a what, but a who, that she *wants* to get into her. Crude, but true.

"No worries, Laney. Just have your lovely self here tonight. I will let Shay know that you are aware of her relationship to Logan, and that you will keep it to yourself. I am sure she will appreciate not having to pretend with at least one person."

"I will see you tonight then."

We say our goodbyes, and I end the call.

Speaking of Shay, I remember that I promised to let her know when I found Logan. I gave her his message, which is an invitation to her parent's for dinner tomorrow. I send her off a quick text, letting her know that I found him, but not where or in what shape. I let her know that the message was delivered, and he said he would talk to her about it tonight. I then send a text to Dante, telling him that I spoke to Laney and all is good. I will fill him in when I see him later.

With all my good deeds done, I am actually looking forward to tonight. It should be entertaining, at the very least.

☺

Saturday nights are always busy, but we have a popular local band playing, and the crowd is quite large. I am a little nervous about how Shay will handle the crowd, but she seems fine. More than fine, really. She is laughing, and seems to be enjoying herself. She is still serving the tables that we assigned to her, but there are a lot more men sitting there, as Dante couldn't screen for us with a crowd this large.

Laney has been giving Logan a hard time, but he doesn't seem to mind, and is smiling like a fool tonight. He was so relieved that she was back, I think that she could do practically anything she wanted to him, and he would just smile through it. He is so far gone over her, and doesn't even know it. What's worse is, Laney seems to be just as ignorant of his interest in her as he is of her interest in him. I can't wait to see what happens when those two trains collide! I am having a silent chuckle over this, when I feel a pair of hands grab my ass.

Normally, I would enjoy this game, but not now when I have a chance with Shay. I quickly turn around, and wish I hadn't.

Kylie's friend is the bun tester.

I can't remember her name. Tara? Tammy? I know it started with a T, but I can't think of it for the life of me. I needn't have worried, as she re-introduces herself.

"Hi there, handsome. Do you remember me? I am Kylie's friend, Trisha. You are looking very delicious tonight."

Two things are very wrong with this. One, I am suffering flashbacks to the, The Incident, and two, I am scanning the club to see if Shay is witnessing this. She is busy with her tables and hasn't noticed. I need to stop this before it goes any further.

"Trisha, it a pleasure to see you again." No, it isn't. "But, I am very busy right now."

"Hmm, you don't look too busy. You are just standing here, looking all lonely." She purrs the last part.

"I assure you that I am doing more than just standing here, and I am not lonely."

"Well, maybe I am the lonely one. Care to go somewhere more private, and help me be less...lonely?"

She has obviously been drinking, and resembles nothing of the woman I remember. Liquid courage is obviously at work here.

"No, thank you, Trisha. I am sure there are plenty of men here tonight who would love the chance to help you with that, but I am not one of them."

I don't like the look she is giving me, it has a malevolent feel to it.

I should have run.

The next thing I know, she reaches her hand out and grabs my penis, hard! All the breath rushes out of me, and my vision goes dim. I desperately try to remove her hand, but her grip is relentless. I am on the verge of tears, and can feel my legs threatening to buckle.

She leans up to me and snarls, "This is for Kylie, you bastard!"

She gives my poor penis one final squeeze, and then releases me.

I drop like a rock.

I am now on the floor, in the fetal position, watching as people rush to the scene.

Perfect, my humiliation is complete. There is a crowd gathered around me.

Trisha is smirking, and is about to slink away, when a body tackles her from the side. It was a blur, so I am not sure who it was. I want to cheer them on, but am having trouble breathing. There is chaos around me now. I can hear yelling and screaming, the crowd is scrambling, and I am pretty sure that I just saw Dante rush towards the commotion. Someone is asking me if I am okay.

Not really!

My penis can't take much more of this abuse!

I realize it is Logan asking me if I am alright. I manage to glance up to him, and the look on my face must have been enough of an answer. He signals to someone, and then I am being gingerly helped to my feet by some of the male staff members. I am not sure which hurts more, my dick, or my ego. People are standing around sucking this all up like sponges, and I think I saw a cell phone camera flash.

Wonderful.

I am being slowly taken to an empty chair when I see what the rest of the crowd is watching. There are two women being restrained by the security staff. One is Terminator Trisha, but I can't believe who the person is who tackled her.

It is Laney, and she is fighting Dante, who is holding her back. She is screaming some pretty creative expletives at The Mangler, Trisha. Trisha has a bloody mouth and the start of a pretty impressive shiner. Her top is ripped on one shoulder at the collar. By the looks of it, Laney kicked her ass! I assess Laney again. Other than looking pissed off, she seems fine.

Way to go, Laney!

Shay is standing beside her now, looking just as pissed off. I try to get her attention, but she is glaring at Trisha, The Worm Wrangler. The security staff member that is holding her, starts to lead her away. She isn't even trying to fight him. I guess Laney knocked it right out of her. Dante takes Laney in the opposite direction, followed by Shay. Logan tells me that the police have been called and should be here shortly.

Oh joy!

I manage to stand on my own, and we head in the direction that Dante took Laney. He has taken her to the security office. When we approach the door, I see her sitting in a chair talking to him. They stop when they notice me standing in the doorway. I manage to hobble into the room and gratefully take the chair that Laney offers, which she was occupying. I gingerly sit, and let out the breath I was holding.

My dick is still throbbing, but isn't as bad as it was. Trisha, The Meat Crusher, must squeeze lemons in her free time because her grip was lethal.

I see that Shay is standing in the corner, and Logan is standing beside her now. Laney comes over to me, and gently leans down and hugs me. I am not sure what I have done to earn this show of emotion from her, but it feels nice and makes me feel a bit better. I can feel the eye-daggers that Logan is throwing at me, but I just don't care. She pulls away, and looks me in the eye.

"I am sorry that I didn't get there sooner, Alex. I took her out when I saw what she did. I had a bad feeling when I saw her talking to you. I just wish I could have done something before she did…well, what she did."

I am blown away by her kindness and sincerity. I wish someone had stopped her sooner too, but that falls on me for letting it get that far, not Laney.

"Please don't blame yourself for what happened. I am extremely grateful to you for thwarting her escape plans. She needs to be dealt with for what she did."

"Damn right she does! I just wish that Dante would have let me finish wiping the floor with her trashy ass."

If I didn't have plans for Shay, and if Logan didn't have feelings for her, I would marry this woman!

"Thank you, Laney. You are now my hero." I manage a weak smile, and she smiles back. She glances at Dante, and then Logan. She clears her throat and asks the obvious question.

"How bad did she hurt you?"

I dip my head to avoid eye contact with anyone.

Laney is the only person in this room that is not aware of my previous injury. I am not sure how to answer this question honestly. After the faith that Laney put in me for telling her the truth about Shay, and now rising to my defense like a conquering hero, I feel she deserves the truth, but am not sure how to begin.

Shay rescues me.

"Her friend Kylie hurt Alex a few nights ago, accidently, and came here earlier today to kiss the boo-boo away, so to speak. Alex declined her offer, and she got pretty hostile. It looks like she shared this with her friend, and the friend decided to get revenge for her slighted girl."

How did Shay know all that?

I look to Logan, but he is staring at the floor.

Loose Lips Louie strikes again!

"Are you serious here? How did the friend of Psycho hurt Alex, and why am I just hearing about all this now?"

She looks more wounded than mad.

I remember the conversation we had earlier on the phone. She doesn't deserve to feel hurt again, so I bite the bullet.

"Laney, it was an injury of a personal nature. Shay only just found out today because she witnessed the scene that took place earlier. No one was keeping secrets from you, because no one knew."

> She slowly loses the hurt expression, and is looking gratefully at me for the honesty. Who knew that my penis would bring us all closer together?

"I understand, and thank you for sharing that with me. It helps me understand why she attacked you. I just assumed it was a lover's quarrel. You guys have quite the rep with the ladies around here, so it was a logical conclusion. Hell, you guys are practically legends!"

I am pretty sure that I am not the only one who is a bit uncomfortable with that. I mean, we have all had very active sex lives, but to have Laney point it out, makes me feel a little dirty. I see that I am not alone, as Dante looks constipated, and Logan is rubbing the back of his neck. Shay looks a little pale, and is deliberately not looking at us. I'm sure that she didn't need to hear that about her cousin, or her potentially new lover, which after tonight might take longer than I was hoping.

Dante's phone alerts him to a message.

He checks his phone, and grimaces.

"Cops are here, boys and girls. Let's move this party to a bigger room."

What did I ever do in a previous life to deserve this?

Chapter Ten

I will spare you the details of what happened with the police.

Everyone wants me to press charges, but I that she will press charges against Laney, and that I don't want. So, in the end, no charges are filed and the police escort Trisha out of the club, with instructions not to return that evening. I could have a restraining order filed against her, but I fear what she might retaliate with.

I am not fit to walk the floors after Trisha's death grip on my member, so I choose to stay in the office for the remainder of the evening. No one is happy with my decision to stay, as they all decide that I should go home. I'm tired of feeling like a child that needs to be coddled. I also need to keep myself occupied, or I'll be more focused on the pain.

It hurts!

Who knew that one, tiny woman could squeeze a dick like a garlic crusher?

I am afraid to look at the new damage to The Big Guy. I am imagining all sorts of horrific scenes in my pants.

I know that I have to look, so I decide to just go for it.

I ease back in the office chair, and proceed to undo my pants. The sound of the zipper sliding down, echoes in the quiet office. I am feeling like a pervert, readying himself for a quick tug, rather than the gruesome inspection I am preparing for. I pause before I reach inside my boxers to retrieve my penis. I am breathing rapidly, and feeling faint. The last thing that I need tonight would be to hyperventilate and pass out with my pants undone, and my cock on display.

Not cool, Alex.

I try to relax, and take some deep breaths. Taking one last deep breath, I whip my dick out. My eyes are drawn downward, against my will.

Oh, for the love of fuck!

My dick now has bruises in the shape of fingerprints down the opposite side of the other bruising. I do believe it also appears to be swollen on both sides now. Honestly, it doesn't even resemble a penis anymore. I feel a sob tear from my throat, and I am mortified to realize that I am crying. As if that wasn't humiliating enough, Logan decides to walk through the door at this moment.

He stops dead in his tracks, and stares at me in complete horror.

"What the hell is that? Please tell me that isn't your dick!"

He hasn't taken his eyes off the mangled flesh between my legs, and I realize that I am actually cradling my former penis now. He has already shut the door, but seems glued to his spot. I can't blame him really. It looks like something out of a horror movie. He finally takes a quick glance at my face, and realizes how upset I am.

"Jesus, Alex. I am so sorry. I am an asshole. I should never have said anything like that. Shit, what can I do to help? Do you want to go back and see that doctor in E.R.?"

No, I really don't.

I am afraid of what he will say, or do, if he sees how bad my penis looks now. I need ice, and my pain pills. I tell Logan this, and he seems relieved to be able to do something. He flies out of the office like zombies are after him, and they realized what a big juicy brain he has.

I surprise myself by having a small chuckle over that mental image. I have no idea what scared him more though, my penis, or my tears. We are guys, and as a rule you don't cry in front of another guy. It's in the rules for carrying your Man Card.

I am still trying to control my pansy-ass tears when the door opens again. I am staring at my crotch, and just assume that it is Logan, back with the ice and some pain medication.

I couldn't have been more wrong.

The moment that I realize it isn't Logan is when I smell her. She always smells so good, like something fresh and clean. I squeeze my eyes shut. There is no point in covering myself now, she has seen the ugly truth.

I try to gingerly put my penis back in my pants, when her words stop me.

"Oh, Alex, please don't. I didn't mean to invade your privacy, but I am so glad that I did. You have no idea what I was imagining the damage looked like. It isn't as bad as I feared, thank goodness!"

I look up at her sharply.

Not as bad as she feared?

What the hell could be worse than this?

With the exception of having it falling off, this is pretty much as bad as it gets!

She must get a sense of what I'm thinking by the look on my face. Her eyes soften, and she smiles gently at me.

"Alex, I know that to you this must seem like the end of the world, but it really isn't. Think of it like any other injury. There is swelling, and bruising, yes, but those will go away. Your penis is mostly just tissue, and will heal like any other tissue damage."

She looks like she is serious right now. I cannot believe that she is standing there, calmly discussing my penis, with a visual aid to boot!

My mouth is gaping, and I honestly don't know how to respond to that.

Fortunately I don't have to, as Logan comes back through the door. He takes in the scene, and then shoots me a stern look.

"Seriously? You couldn't have put it away by now, and especially in the presence of my cousin?"

He goes to move past Shay, but she turns and stops him.

"Your cousin has seen a penis before and does not need you to protect her delicate sensibilities! I asked him not to cover himself when I walked in, because he was rushing to do just that and might have hurt himself further. I am going to be dating your friend, cousin, and I would have seen his penis at some point!" She says all this in a menacing whisper while leaning up-close to Logan's face.

He looks appalled, but also chastised.

I am a little uncomfortable about them discussing my penis so openly. I look down at my lap again.

Am I being overly dramatic about how I am seeing my dick like Shay said?

I didn't think so, but I look at myself and try to see the damage as Shay described. I know there might be another injury below the surface that she is unaware of, so I look at the surface injuries. Bruising and swelling, with a slight bend.

Nope, not being overly dramatic.

It is a nightmare!

"Shay, can we please not discuss this? I have some ice for Alex, and some pain meds. Would you allow me to come in, so that I can give them to him?"

He is being overly polite, and I know that this means he isn't happy.

Shay nods her head and moves aside so he can pass. He stalks over to me and slaps an ice pack down on the desk beside me, along with a bottle of Motrin that he must have gotten from somewhere. He doesn't even look at me, just turns around and briskly leaves the office, shutting the door behind him.

I am guessing that he still isn't thrilled with the idea of Shay and I being together.

Well, too bad!

I reach over for the ice pack and realize that I am still on display. I put my dick back in my pants, but don't bother zipping up. I reach for the ice pack again, and place it on my groin.

Oh, sweet relief!

"Let me get you some water to swallow those pills down with. I will be right back."

I thank her for that. She just waves me off, and then hurries from the room. I tip my head back and begin to relax slightly as the ice pack works its magic.

A few minutes later, I hear the office door open yet again. I smell her, and smile. I bring my head forward and look up into a pair of sapphire eyes smiling down on me.

God, please let me keep her?

"I got you some water. How many pills do you need to take?" She reaches down and brushes a piece of hair from my forehead.

I think I let out a sigh.

"Just two should do for now."

She pops the lid off the bottle and shakes out two pills that she then hands to me. I gratefully accept them and pop them in my mouth. She hands me the water next, and I take a swig. She is chewing her lip, and I am dying to soothe it with my tongue. She takes the bottle from me and places it on the desk. She then perches her delectable derriere on the edge, and takes a deep breath before she speaks.

"Listen to me, Alex. This doesn't change anything for me. I am still extremely attracted to you, and I still plan on going out to lunch with you. The only thing this changes is the time frame of when we become intimate. I am perfectly happy to spend time with you, in any capacity. I do not want you to feel rushed into having sex with me before you are healed. We will take this slowly, and see how everything plays out. Hear me well though, regardless of your injuries, what I saw just now confirms for me how much I want you. Sex is definitely going to happen between us, Big Boy." She then winks at me.

Oh. My. God!

Did you hear that, Big Guy? She was talking about you!

She wants us!

I have never been so touched and turned on at the same time.

God is good!

She is waiting for me to acknowledge what she said.

Oh baby, Daddy is a happy man!

"You have no idea how badly I needed to hear that. I am glad to hear that you want this as much as I do. Honestly, I don't think I have ever wanted anything more."

That is a huge understatement. I want this so badly, but not just for the sex, and that is new for me.

I have never felt the need to get to know a woman more than in the biblical sense. I am entering new territory here. I have to wonder if I would have just tried to sleep with her, regardless of what I told Logan. Mutual gratification is usually all I am interested in offering a woman, but I find myself wanting to give Shay so much more.

We share a smile, and then something in me shifts. I reach up and gently grasp the back of her neck, and slowly bring her head down towards mine. I am staring into her eyes, watching for any sign that she doesn't want this. All I see is an eagerness that matches my own. When our lips are just a breath apart, I take a moment to anticipate the feel of her plump lips cushioning my own. She surprises me by letting out a little whimper, and then closing the final distance between us.

Nothing could have prepared me for the impact of that kiss. Quite honestly, I felt it in every fiber of my being.

I know that sounds cliché, but it is the truth.

When her lips brushed against mine, I felt a shiver that coursed through my whole body. She teases me with her luscious lips for a few more beats, before I decide to change the game.

I have always been a bit of an alpha, so being passive during this exchange was not going to happen. I slide my tongue into play, and lick her lips. She lets out a little gasp, and that is the opening that I needed. I lean forward to deepen the kiss, and change the angle of her head for a better fit. She moans, and then brings her own tongue into the exchange.

I think I moaned myself at that.

It is perfect, and would have continued to be perfect, if my penis hadn't decided to respond to the adrenal rush I was enjoying. He begins to engorge, and I wince.

Shay notices, and breaks the kiss.

Nooooo! Come back lips!

I think I hear a whimper, and I am not sure whether it is from my penis, or myself. I get some satisfaction from the fact that Shay is breathing heavily, and looking a little dazed. Also, I can't help but notice that her nipples are poking out through her uniform.

This time I know that it is me who whimpers.

Shay looks down, realizes what I am distressed over, and laughs. I reach over and snag her hand. She has such soft, dainty hands. I tell her how badly I have wanted to do that, and she says that it has been the same for her. We share a smile and agree that we are both eager for Tuesday to arrive. She then reminds me that she needs to be back on the floor, and I reluctantly let her go. I watch her walk towards the door. She turns and sends me a smile over her shoulder, and then leaves me alone in the office.

Tuesday can't come soon enough!

Chapter Eleven

I will jump ahead a few days to, "Date Day."

I barely made it through the few days leading up to today. I was becoming a tad obsessive about making sure that everything was perfect for our first official date. I want to romance her with style. I booked us a table at the nicest restaurant in town, I had my baby detailed and waxed, I bought a new suit, and I even went and got my hair trimmed and styled.

Logan and Dante may have had too much fun with me over this, the assholes.

I usually have my prowess in the bedroom to fall back on, but alas, she will have to wait to be wowed by me between the sheets. I am feeling optimistic about the wow factor happening though, as The Big Guy is improving nicely. He even managed a full-on erection this morning!

That has to be a good sign, right?

So, here we are. It is Tuesday, and I am pulling up in front of her house. She still lives with her parents, and I am a tad nervous about this. I have met her parents before, but not as a suitor.

I will be honest, her dad scares me a little.

He is a monster of a man, and he is also a lawyer. Logan's dad, and Shay's dad are brothers, but you wouldn't know it to look at them. Logan's dad is tall and wiry, with golden blonde hair and green eyes. Shay's dad is a wall of muscle, with light brown hair and the same blue eyes that Shay has. He could put a hurt on me, and he'd be able to make sure that the law is on his side.

Not happy thoughts.

Her mom is a sweetheart, and Shay looks just like her. I am hoping that I can appeal to her so that she can help smooth the way.

I am out of my car, and approaching the door. Before I can put my hand up to knock, the door is slowly, and menacingly, opened. I am frozen to the spot, as over six feet of mind and muscle is staring back at me. Her dad doesn't move, just glares at me from the other side of the threshold. I clear my throat, and extend my hand to him, as I cringe in fear on the inside.

"Hello, Mr. Crawford. I am here to collect Shayla for our date."

I think I managed that without sounding as scared as I feel. There are only five years between Shayla and myself, but with the way that her dad is looking at me, I feel like a pervert here to violate his child. He raises an eyebrow at me, but otherwise remains the same. I can feel myself starting to perspire, and the last thing that I want for my date is to be a hot, sweaty mess.

Christ, I feel like a teenager!

He takes a step through the door, and gently closes it behind him, while facing me.

"I know why you are here, and I know that you are a friend of Logan's, but you are no friend of mine. You need to earn my respect, boy. I cannot stop her from making her own decisions, but I know ways of making sure that those decisions don't hurt her. If she is just an itch that you need to scratch, I suggest that you find yourself a scratching post."

I can't say that I am too shocked by this outpouring of the warm and fuzzies, but I am getting tired of everyone assuming the worst of me where Shay is concerned.

"Mr. Crawford, I can assure you that my intentions towards your daughter are honest. I just want to be given the opportunity to date her and get to know her."

He seems to mull this over, and take a deeper assessment of me. "Fine, but just so we are clear, if you hurt her, you and I will have a problem."

I sigh and reply, "Logan already threatened me too, so please believe me when I say that I have no intentions of hurting her."

This seems to intrigue him. "I need to thank Logan for that then. Alright, I think we understand each other. I will go and get Shayla now."

I take my first proper breath as he heads back inside. This time he leaves the door open, and I can see the stairs that lead up to the second story from the hallway, and that is when I see her.

She is just starting to descend the stairs and hasn't noticed me yet. She is staring questioningly at her father. She is wearing a black dress that is hugging her every curve and matching black heels. Her hair is down and loose upon her shoulders with slight curls at the bottom. She is so beautiful that she steals the breath I just took. I look to her father just as his head turns towards me, and the damned eyebrow goes up again. I must look like an idiot standing here ogling his daughter in front of him.

I am not winning any points right now, and he looks like a score-keeper.

I swing my gaze back up to Shay, and see that she has noticed me. She has a tiny smile on her face, which I hope means she likes what she sees.

I am wearing my new, black suit, custom tailored, with new, black, dress shoes and a gold and black tie.

Yes, I said tie.

I am making huge sacrifices for this girl.

My hair is slightly shorter, and styled. Her smile gets bigger as she gets closer to me. I am desperate to reach out and see if her hair is as soft as it looks right now, but I don't think that Daddy Dearest would approve. Instead, I take her delicate hand, and raise it to my lips. I barely allow my lips to make contact with her skin, as we are being watched. She blushes slightly, and then turns towards her father.

"Bye, Daddy. I am not sure what Alex has planned for us, but I will let you know when I will be home."

She then turns back around and doesn't see him point at his eyes, and then at me. I wouldn't be surprised if he has spies around the city, so that he can keep his eyes on me.

Not a comfortable thought.

I keep her hand in mine, and nod towards her father while I gently steer her away from the house.

Once I have her at the car, I gallantly open the door for her and reach inside to retrieve the single, red rose that I have waiting for her on the seat. I straighten and hand the rose over to her. Her whole face lights up as she accepts my offering. She slowly lifts up on her toes, and gently kisses me on the cheek. I can feel eyes burning the back of my head, but I don't care. My skin is tingling from where her lips have just been, and I am smiling like a fool. I help her into my baby, and carefully close the door. I feel like skipping around the car, but I manage to restrain myself. Once I am in the car, I chance a quick glance at Shay. She is cradling her rose, and smiling down at it.

Score one for The Puddle Maker!

I can keep score too.

It's a relatively quiet drive to the restaurant, but not uncomfortable. She asks where we are going, so I tell her. She seems excited, and admits she has always wanted to eat there. I also tell her that I have plans for after lunch, and she's eager to hear about what I have planned, but that I want to keep it a surprise. She asks about my baby, which I'm more than happy to tell her all about. She makes a comment about boys and their toys, but admits that my baby is a nice toy.

My girls are now friends.

When we arrive, I get out of the car first, so that I can open her door for her again. She seems charmed by this, which is what I'm hoping for, but it is also how my mother raised me. Respect for women and manners were drilled into me from an early age. Both my parents are very British, one being, Scottish and the other, Welsh. I was raised with a very strict sense of morals and ethics, hence the gentleman slut. I am sure my parents would die if they knew about that though, so we can just keep it to ourselves. I am almost positive that my mother still believes I am a virgin, even after catching me with several girls, in precarious situations, growing up. She probably has herself convinced that they were taking advantage of me, even though I was a willing victim.

We are now seated at our table, and waiting for our food. We agree to share an appetizer, before our meal arrives. There is a candle on the table, and it is reflecting in her eyes, making them shimmer like precious gems. She has the most amazing eyes I have ever seen on a woman. Her lashes are almost black, and so thick that they resemble a fringe. I could wax poetic about them some more, but there are other features that need to be worshipped as well.

Her lips are still pornographically plump, but I am finding my thoughts focusing more on making them smile, instead of wrapping them around my dick, or sucking on them. She has a radiant smile that lights up her whole face. Her hair is dark and glossy, and even as I picture it spread out on my pillow, I am also imagining what it will feel like if I reach over, and caress one of her curls.

What is happening to me?

Is it because my pecker is out of commission that I am able to focus on more than sex with a woman, or is it something about Shay? Whatever it is, I have never felt this way around a woman before, and I think that I like it.

I like it a lot.

Our appetizer arrives, and we make small talk while we nibble. I am completely relaxed, and captivated by the woman before me. She tells me about some articles that she has worked on for her magazine, and how much she enjoys her job. I share some funny stories about the club, and the guys. I also share with her my suspicions about Logan, and Laney. She says that she suspects Logan won't admit his feelings, and that unless Laney throws her feelings in his face, he will continue to live in denial. I have suspected something in Logan's past has made him this way, and ask Shay if she knows what it is. She tells me that she only knows bits and pieces, as she was so young when it happened, but that it was his story to tell. I have to respect her loyalty. Actually, I am coming to realize there is a lot to respect about this woman. She also confides in me that she has her eye on an apartment that she wants to move into, but is having trouble finding the courage to tell her dad. I can only imagine how that conversation will go down, and don't envy her that. She assures me that her father isn't unreasonable, but tends to be overly protective of her.

Really? That is an understatement, I believe.

She claims that she is going to try to tell him this weekend, as it is her parents' anniversary, and he wouldn't dare make her mother upset by refusing their daughter something and causing a scene on their special day.

Hmm, it appears that Shay has a sneaky streak as well. Good to know.

After we have finished our meal, I tell Shay that we will be leaving here, and proceeding to our second part of the date. She asks again where we are going, and again I refuse to disclose our next destination. She actually pouts at this, and I can't resist leaning in and stealing a quick kiss. I hear the little gasp that escapes her lips, and smile to myself.

Oh yes, she will be mine.

Let part two of the date commence.

Chapter Twelve

The second part of the date is the part that I hope will impress her the most. I found out from Logan that she is an art enthusiast. I spend quite a bit of money and called in some favors for this part. We arrive at the Museum of Modern Art, and I watch as her whole face lights up.

Score another point for me.

"The museum, Alex! How did you know that this is one of my favorite places?" she asks while practically bouncing in her seat.

I smile at her, but on the inside I am doing a happy dance of my own over her excitement.

"A little birdie might have been bribed to disclose the information."

I take her hand and lift it to my lips. I linger over it, inhaling the scent of her skin. She is stunning, sitting here in my car and looking at me like I just hung the moon for her. If she is impressed now, she is in for a treat once she gets inside.

I release her hand and exit the car. Once I have her carefully out of my baby, I take her hand and we ascend the stairs leading to the front doors. I love the way her hand feels in mine, and I find myself stroking her skin with my thumb. We enter through the massive doors that lead into the main lobby. My minion at the museum is waiting for us. He approaches and bows towards Shay. Once he straightens, he informs us that they have been expecting us and tells us to please follow him.

Shay looks over at me with bewilderment on her face, but I just smile and nod at her. At this, she seems to clue in to the fact that something is going on, and raises her eyebrow at me, smiling seductively.

Damn! The Big Guy must have seen that, as he is now swelling in my pants. There is no way for me to discreetly adjust myself at this point, so I tug on her hand and follow behind my minion.

We turn several corners, and pass most of the main galleries. I can feel myself getting more excited with each step. We finally arrive at our destination. My minion stops before a door that leads into one of the private galleries. I chance a look at Shay, but she isn't looking at me. I look back towards my minion, and give him the nod that he may proceed. With a grand flourish, he opens the door and steps aside for us. I hear a gasp from beside me, and I smile to myself. I place my hand on her lower back and usher her in first. There is another gasp, and then she stops to take it all in.

I have to admit, it looks amazing.

I asked the gallery if I could rent this private room for a few hours and have some of the art arranged in it. The art in the room is by an artist that Shay is supposed to be a big fan of. Between each display is a single, red rose in a vase. At the end of the room, there is a table with fresh fruit, cheese, breads and champagne chilling in a tub. The centerpiece of the table is the remainder of the roses, arranged in an artful vase.

You are in awe of me, are you not?

I know that I am!

I have never put this much effort into a date, or impressing a woman before. I should feel nervous, but all I am feeling is pride over my efforts.

Shay is still trying to take it all in, and she is wandering around the room. She finally stops at the table with her back to me. She takes a few minutes, before she turns towards me. This time I gasp, for there are tears running unchecked down her cheeks.

Okay, now I'm panicked!

I am about to rush to her, when she speaks.

"Alex, I can honestly say that no one has ever done anything like this for me before. I am overwhelmed. My favorite art, the private room to view them, the romantic setting, and the beautiful flowers. You have no idea how much I love all of this, and how touched I am that you have done all this for me. I want to say thank you, but that doesn't seem to be enough for all that you have done here today."

She is still crying, and I am confused. If she is happy, why is she still crying?

I walk carefully towards her. Once I reach her, I can't help but reach out and wipe the tears from her eyes. She smiles up at me, but I can see that her eyes are still moist. Not knowing what else to do, I lean down towards her. I am going slowly, and allowing her to see the emotions in my own eyes. Her eyes close just before I reach her lips, and I finish my decent. I brush my lips softly over hers, testing their willingness. She rubs her plump lips back against mine, and opens them slightly. I lick lightly along her lips, and encourage her to open just a bit wider. She does, and I tip my head for a better fit, before I seal out mouths together. This kiss is even better than the one we shared the other night. I swear I hear angels singing in the distance, it is that pure.

I didn't know that I had this in me!

I don't want to cheapen the moment, so I gently pull away from her lips. I lean back, and notice that her eyes are still closed and moist. I don't know what is coming over me, but I lean over and kiss each of her eyes, trying to erase her tears. She sighs, and when I am finished and leaning back, she opens them.

I am knocked off my feet by the emotion I see in her eyes.

I have never had a woman look at me the way she is now.

I feel a lump forming in my throat, and am not sure how to process all that I am feeling. She is making me feel things that I have never felt before. She then reaches up and strokes her soft fingers down my cheek. She is smiling, and it is as gentle and beautiful as she is. This woman doesn't know the power that she has over me. I would do just about anything to see that look on her face, aimed at me, for the rest of my life.

Did you hear that?

I just spoke about forever in regards to a woman!

My mother was right, the perfect woman can change everything.

I am still reeling from all this, when Shay takes a deep breath and grasps my hand.

"You have no idea what all this means to me. This is the most perfect moment of my life, and I owe that to you. You are an amazing man, Alex Bradley."

"You deserve the best, Shay. I hope to get the opportunity to show you that there is so much more that I can do to make you happy."

Listen to the mushy words, flowing out of my mouth.

Who is this man?

Whoever he is, his words seem to be working. Shay wraps her arms around me, and my breath is rushing out of me at the unexpected move. Damn, the woman is soft in all the right places.

"I am happy just being with you. You had better be careful, or I won't let you go…ever." She whispers the last word, like she is unsure of whether she should have voiced it. I gently squeeze her to me to let her know that I heard it and I am perfectly fine with that.

To be honest, I am feeling more than fine with that.

Shouldn't that scare a man-whore like me?

We discuss her favorite art pieces, eat some of the food, and sip on champagne. It's an amazing afternoon. Shay is smart, funny and endearing. I could have spent all day just listening to her talk and sharing her company, which is a first for me. Usually the only conversation I enjoy with a woman is the one that leads to sex. There will be no sex at the end of this date, and I am miraculously okay with that. Don't get me wrong here, if The Big Guy was fully functional, I would be trying to steer the date in that direction. I am a guy!

  We pack up the flowers for her to take home, and leave the rest for my minion to take care of. Don't feel bad for him, he was paid well for it. I'm a little afraid of what might be waiting for me when I take her home. Her dad could be devising all forms of torture for me and my member. Like I said before, he scares me. I pray that I never give him reason to inflict bodily damage on me. I have no intentions of ever hurting Shay, but some things are out of my control and I don't know what the future holds. I take a deep breath as I pull up in front of her house. It's around dinner time now, and I'm hoping for a quick escape. I walk Shay to her door like a gentlemen. She thanks me for the amazing date, lifts her flowers up to her nose and delicately sniffs them. I lean down, give her a kiss on her cheek, and promise to text her later to discuss plans for another date. She opens the front door and I hold my breath. I don't see any hulking figure waiting on the other side, and release my breath. Shay turns and smiles at me. I take this as my cue to leave, and turn and walk back to the car. I wave to her over the top before I get in. That is when I see the sinister shadow in the living-room window. Taking this as my sign to get out of Dodge, I quickly jump into my baby and we exit down the street.

How do you win a father over? My very life might depend on this, so I had better figure that one out quickly.

Chapter Thirteen

"How do you win a father's approval?" I ask Dante. I decide to talk to him first about my dilemma.

He looks appalled by the question. "Why would I want a father's approval to have sex with his daughter? Do I look suicidal?"

I should have known better, but I have gone too far with this line of questioning to turn back now. "No, but I want his approval to date her, not molest her."

"I have never had to impress a father before. I guess you could always try having a man-to-man with him, or maybe find what his interests are, and appeal to him that way."

He must be thinking too hard about this, because he is starting to look constipated.

"I have, unfortunately, had a man-to-mouse moment with him, and it wasn't Hallmark quality. Finding out what his interests are isn't a bad idea, though. I'll have to ask Logan what he likes."

Dante and I are at a local pub having a late bite to eat. We like the atmosphere here, and it is close to work. I also asked Logan to join us, but he has yet to arrive.

I am playing with the label on my bottle of beer and reflecting on my date with Shay. I know that I have a dopey smile on my face, but I don't care. It was everything that I hoped it would be and I can't seem to stop myself from grinning.

"I am guessing by the look on your face that, aside from the father, the date went well?"

I look up at Dante and just nod my head. They were a vital part of the planning process, but I don't want to share the intimate details of my date with my friends. I know that they will want them, but they are mine.

"Thank you for all your help. It was perfect, and she absolutely loved it."

"No worries, my man. Now we just need to figure out a way past her dad, and you are golden." He snags his beer, and takes a drink.

I have the best friends.

I really do.

I hear the bell above the door chime, and look over to see Logan coming through. This pub doesn't cater to a young crowd, and it is filled with mostly male patrons, but the few cougars that are here all swivel to watch him approach our table.

I laugh to myself.

It never gets old watching the looks on women's faces when they lay eyes on him for the first time. He really is a god among men, yet his head is down here with the rest of us. Logan does not have an over-inflated ego to match his looks. Quite the opposite, in fact. He seems embarrassed and frustrated by it most of the time. Today he is ignoring the looks he is receiving and just takes his seat with us, as if every eye in the place isn't on him. Even the men can't help themselves.

Priceless.

"Alright ladies, what were we talking about before I got here?"

He signals the waiter over, and the poor guy almost trips over a chair, in his rush to get to him.

Honestly, he is just a man people!

"Well, it seems that operation, 'Win the Girl,' went off without a hitch. Only problem seems to be her dad." Dante puts his bottle back on the table, and waits for Logan to place his order, before he continues. "Any idea how he can win your uncle over?"

Logan rubs the back of his neck. Not a good sign. "Uncle Mike is a hard man to warm-up to. I love the guy, and have a lot of respect for him. If it wasn't for his help, my family would have ended-up on the streets." He shudders at the memory. "He had to become tough, and ruthless in his field in order to get to the top, and I guess that has made him jaded and cautious around people."

Great, that is not what I wanted to hear.

I already knew most of that. But I want some insight into his more human side, not the side I already have the displeasure of knowing. He must see my dejection, and tries to give me better advice.

"Well, he likes soccer and he plays with his friends every Sunday. Maybe you could accidentally, on purpose, be at the park where they play?"

I just stare at him.

Surely he is not implying that I play soccer with his uncle? I am injured, and would be exposing myself as an open target on a field, where there would be a large ball...and a large man...with large feet.

I can just see it now.

Picture it...

Me, running with my penis slapping against my leg, causing further damage, and pain. Her dad, kicking the ball towards my crotch, possibly maiming me for life. Or he just says, "Screw the ball!" and just uses his foot to make sure that I don't ever get the opportunity to violate his daughter.

I don't think so!

"Actually that isn't a bad idea. Just show up to watch, and possibly cheer him on. Make an even better impression, by bringing his daughter to watch him play." Dante is nodding his head like this makes perfect sense.

I really don't want to spend a date with Shay watching old, jiggly men play soccer.

"Nah, Shay isn't into soccer. She wouldn't want to hang with her dad and his friends, watching them kick a ball around. I say that you go yourself and try to make it obvious that you are making an effort to get to know him, outside of his daughter." Logan accepts his beer from the waiter and takes a huge swallow. "So, other than my uncle, you and Shay are okay?" He looks like he struggled with a lemon to say that last part, as his face is all puckered.

I growl to myself.

Looks like I have more than just her dad to convince, that I am a different man with Shay, and that I deserve a chance.

"Yes, we are okay. Better than okay, really. I feel different when I am around her. She makes me want things that I never have before. I just want to make her smile, and listen to her voice. She is so amazing, and I find myself thinking about her all the time."

There is silence at our table.

I look from one to the other of them, and they are both staring at me. Dante is looking at me in, dare I say, longing. I know that deep down he is a softie, and probably wants a good woman too, he just hides it well. Logan on the other hand, is looking at me with disbelief.

That hurts.

Dante recovers first.

"Well, it seems that you are serious about this one. I hope it all works out for you then. I like Shay, always have. She would be good for you."

I am not sure how to take that.

Does that mean that I wouldn't be good for her?

Well, screw that!

"I would be good for her too. I am getting tired of everyone making me out to be a bad guy. Just because I haven't wanted to become serious with anyone until now, doesn't mean that I didn't want that for myself. Also, I have always treated women with respect, and been a gentleman around them. I have a lot of qualities a woman would enjoy, besides my dick!" I may have shouted that last part.

I look around the pub, and sure enough, everyone is staring openly at me.

I hang my head.

What is wrong with me lately?

If I didn't know it was impossible, I would think that I had P.M.S.

Seriously, why am I so sensitive lately?

I just don't know.

I hear a throat being cleared, and look over at Logan. He makes sure that he has my full attention before he begins.

"Alex, I never wanted you to feel like a bad guy. I am being a jerk to you over this, and I am sorry. I think of Shayla like a sister, and you guys are like my brothers. It just feels a bit awkward, and uncomfortable for me, is all. I have known you for eleven years now, and I know pretty much everything about you. I know you are a decent guy, but until now, you were only interested in a woman long enough for her to orgasm. I just didn't want Shay to expect more from you and get hurt. It appears that I was wrong though, and for that I am sorry. I will be better about this from now on. Just do me a favor and not discuss your sex life with me when the time comes. There is only so much I can handle."

I can accept that.

I lean over for a fist bump, and we are all good.

I still want to make him suffer a bit for what he has put me through, so I don't feel any guilt, right now, over bringing up the next subject.

"So, how are you and Laney?"

Logan was about to take a drink, but stops halfway to his mouth. He calmly puts the bottle back on the table, but keeps his eyes on it while he answers. "What do you mean?"

I look over to Dante, who is smirking. Looks like we are going to have to be blunt. "I mean the attraction that is between the two of you?"

"There is no attraction. She is an employee."

"An employee that you have the hots for." Dante doesn't have any problem putting it out there.

Logan finally looks up at us. "I do not have the hots for her. She is an employee, and a friend. That is all."

Shay was right, he won't admit it. I look to Dante, who is just staring at Logan.

I was not prepared for what happens next.

"Then it shouldn't matter to you that one of the bartenders asked her out the other night? She said, yes," Dante continued.

He says this so matter-of-factly, when it is anything but. I don't know whether this is true or not, but I think the shit just hit the fan.

Logan's face starts to darken. "Which one?"

Dante just shrugs. "Mark, our head bartender."

Uh oh!

Logan already had to tell that weenie off about how he was ogling Shay, and I know there have been other times he has bumped heads with him. I can see by the look on Logan's face that he is remembering all this too. His eye is starting to twitch.

"We have a no-dating policy."

For someone who looks like he could commit murder, he is being eerily quiet.

Not a good sign.

"You seem to be the only one hung-up on that. We can't control what they do in their free time, or with whom. As long as it doesn't interfere with their jobs, I could care less."

I happen to agree with Dante, but choose to wisely remain quiet.

"Why have rules at all then, if no one is going to follow them?" Logan's eye is twitching faster now.

"Calm down, man. That is the only rule that has been broken, and personally, I think it is a bad rule. If you tell someone they can't do something in their personal life, it is only going to make them want to do it more. As for Laney, she is a beautiful woman. Sooner or later, some guy is going to sweep her off her feet."

Wow, Dante has some brass balls!

I would not have had the guts to wave the red flag in front of Logan like that. His eye isn't just twitching now, it is bulging out of his face. Logan is gritting his teeth when he answers.

"I am aware of her beauty, and her rights to date, just like anyone else. Why do you seem to think that it is my concern? If the rule wasn't there, would I have approached her? Yes, but only long enough to get a good, hard fuck out of her! Is that what you wanted to hear?"

Both Dante and I are stunned by this. Maybe we pushed him into saying that, because Logan would never speak so disrespectfully about anyone, especially Laney.

He grabs his wallet and tosses some bills on the table, then gets up and storms out of the pub.

I don't feel very good about myself right now.

We were only trying to get him to open up, as any good friends would. I did not expect that reaction.

What did we just do?

Chapter Fourteen

Later that night, I am lying in bed, replaying all the events of the day. It was the best day of my life, yet one of the worst too. My date with Shay was without a doubt, the best time I have had with a woman, including all my sexcapades. If just being in her company can make me feel this way, I cannot wait to see what I feel when I finally have her in my bed. My penis agrees, and salutes me from under the sheet. I am encouraged by its enthusiasm that this will be happening, and possibly soon. I know the doctor said to wait two weeks, but how am I going to know if I am okay, unless I plug my equipment in?

Yes, that was a metaphor for sex.

I am concerned about Logan though. He hasn't answered any of my calls or texts. Dante has tried too, but hasn't heard from him either. We feel horrible about the way things ended at the pub. I can't imagine what Logan was feeling, to just blurt out what he did. I hope that he is okay, and doesn't do something stupid, like drink his misery away again. I should probably let Shay know what happened. I promised to text her later this evening to make plans for another date anyways.

I reach over to the nightstand and grab my cell phone.

Hi beautiful. What are you doing?

She replies almost instantly.

Just watching TV. U?

Lying in bed and thinking of you ;-)

Is the winking face too much?

Maybe.

Charmer :-)

Yes I am.

Should I tell her about Logan first, or make plans for another date? I guess I should go with the bad first.

Actually, have some news about Logan.

Really? What is it?

We may have pushed him about Laney. Didn't go over well.

Oh no! Is he ok?

He won't answer us. Getting worried.

> **Will try him. Gimme a sec.**

I am hoping that she can get him to talk to her. I will feel better knowing that he is okay.

Several minutes go by, and I am just about to text her not to bother, when my phone beeps at me. I assume it is Shay, but it is Logan.

> **Asshole. I am fine.**

Okay, at least I know he is alive, and sounding like himself. I type a quick text back to him, telling him to call me in the morning. He just answers with the letter, K.

Typical.

I then text Dante to let him know that Logan is okay. Dante doesn't answer, but I am not worried about him. He is probably just busy, with a woman.

Shay texts me next.

> **Done. He is at home. Didn't say much though :-(**

I didn't think he would, but at least he answered her.

Ty. You are an angel.

Flattery will get U everything ;-)

I smile to myself, enjoying the banter.

Everything U say? Hmmmm...I have a few ideas.

Naughty boy. I am sure U do.

She has no idea!

How about that next date?

What did U have in mind?

Well, I was planning another romantic gesture, but maybe I should see what ideas she has.

What does the lady like?

Oh, ladies choice is it?

If the lady wishes.

Let me think here...

I smile, as I picture her chewing on that lip, deep in thought. She also scrunches her nose slightly when she is thinking.

So adorable.

I am so lost in thought that I don't notice my phone has gone off. I quickly scan it to see what she has said. I laugh out loud with what she texted.

Fishing?

I don't know if she is serious or not, but either way, she has delighted me. I quickly reply.

Really?

Yes, silly. I have always loved to fish. You and me, in a boat, on a lake, alone. Sound good?

I think I just swooned.

This woman is slowly stealing my heart. How perfect would a quiet day of fishing be? I am so on board with that! I would never have pegged her as a lover of fishing, but I am learning that there is so much more to her than I would have thought. I can't wait to discover everything. I tell her that it sounds perfect, and I will make all the arrangements tomorrow, and then let her know when we are going.

Ok. Night Alex <3

I stare at the screen for a few moments. I want to type something awesome, but nothing comes to mind. I have to type something though, before she starts to wonder why I am not responding.

> **Sleep well, sweet Shay. I will dream of you.**

Charmer :-) Same here

Perfect!

The next day, I shoot out of bed with renewed purpose. I have a fishing trip to arrange, and a friend to fix.

I rush through my morning routines, and I am out the door in record time. I decide not to take my baby out today, and opt for the S.U.V. instead. I decide that Logan needs my attention first, so I drive over to his place. The three of us all live fairly close to each other, and the club. Logan and I own condos, whereas Dante just rents a flat.

I park in the visitor parking spot for his condo, and ride the elevator up to his floor. I am hoping that he actually answers the door for me. I have a key, but I don't want to use it. I exit the elevator and walk down the hall to his door which is at the very end. I listen carefully first for any noise coming from within that might tell me what is happening on the other side. All is quiet, so I raise my hand and knock. I wait for a few minutes. No response. I raise my hand to knock again, when I hear shuffling from the other side. There is the sound of locks being disengaged, and then the door swings open.

Logan is standing in the doorway, looking like hell. He has on the same pants from yesterday, minus his shirt. His hair looks like he has been running his fingers through it all night, and his eyes have some serious baggage underneath. I am guessing that he hasn't had much sleep, if any. He is just glaring at me. I start to shift on my feet, not knowing how to proceed. He turns around and stalks away, but leaves the door open. I take this as a sign that I may enter, and do so. I shut the door behind me and go in search of him. I don't have to travel far, as he is sitting on his couch staring out the window.

Logan has a spectacular living room. Everything has a specific place and it is all displayed to perfection. His home is very sterile which is why the one thing that is out of place is glaringly obvious. There, on the table, is a scarlet-red, lace bra. I stop dead in my tracks. Usually where there is clothing, there is a body that wears it. I look around the rest of the room. Nothing else seems out of place, and there is no further evidence that a woman is somewhere nearby, minus her bra. I strain my ears for any sound coming from the other rooms that might hint another person is here, but all is silent. Well, either she is a dead, or she is already gone.

Yeah, my guess is she is gone.

I slowly approach the opposite side of the couch and lower myself down. Not sure what to do next, so I decide to just dive in with my apology speech.

"Look, I know that it was an asshole move that we pulled on you yesterday. I am sorry, and so is Dante. We never would have brought it up if we knew how you would react. I don't know what has made you so closed off to the possibility of more with a woman, but I do know that you deserve more than what you seem to think is enough for you."

He is still sitting silently beside me, and he hasn't even acknowledged that I have spoken. I am just about to leave him to whatever hell he is in, when he starts to speak.

"It doesn't matter. I made a mistake years ago, and this is all I have left to offer a woman. I was so mad yesterday, at you, Dante, what he told me, Laney, all of it. I tried to lose myself the only way I know how, with sex, but I couldn't follow through."

I don't know what to say to this.

Does he mean he couldn't, as in physically, or wouldn't, because of where his head was? I didn't have to wonder long.

"Don't get that look on your face, it wasn't that I was unable to perform. Everything was working, I just couldn't get my head into it. That made me even madder. I ended up sending the girl home, in a cab. Let's just say, that she was not impressed with the way the evening ended. I am guessing that my rep is about to be ruined, but I just don't care. I found the bra under the table, and I have just been staring at it since." He looks at me now.

There is so much grief in his eyes, I feel a little choked-up myself.

How can I help my friend?

We have all watched him become more withdrawn lately, but no one has been able to find out what the reason is.

"Why do you think you couldn't follow through?"

He laughs, but it is filled with anger. He gets up and starts to pace.

Finally, he stops and swivels towards me. "That is the question, isn't it? If I knew the answer to that, I wouldn't be such a mess right now, would I?"

I don't think he was really looking for an answer, but I give him one anyways. "I think that you feel more for Laney than you want to, or are willing to."

He hangs his head, and slumps his shoulders. "I can't feel anything for her. I won't. I have nothing to offer her. She deserves more than I can give her, but it is driving me insane that someone else might. I felt horrible about what I said in the pub, and tried to prove to myself that a fuck is the only thing I can offer her. It didn't work, and made me feel even worse. Please, just let the whole Laney thing go. I can't go there."

His eyes are pleading with me, so I nod my head in agreement. But silently, I vow that in time I will see my broken friend fixed.

Chapter Fifteen

I end up at the club later that day. I need to find a phone number for a contact that we have who also owns a boat. Okay, so he owns a small yacht. I make a deal with him to use his yacht for the day. I know that Shay works mostly freelance, so I was hoping that Monday would be good for her. I don't like making plans for the nights that we are busy with the club or the following days. I would have liked to do this sooner, but it can't be helped. I also call our kitchen manager to see if he can help me with food for the day like he did for me on the first date. He's a little too eager to help, carrying on about 'young love'. Our kitchen manager thinks that because he is French, he knows all about the affairs of the heart. He is a wonderful chef and manager, but also a hopeless romantic. He has been with us since the beginning, and has constantly been after us to settle down with "nice girls." He was practically in tears when I asked him for his help with the last date, and by the sounds he was making on the phone, this time isn't going to be any different. He says he feels like a proud papa, helping one of his boys get the girl of their dreams. She is definitely the girl of my fantasies, but I am also starting to believe she is more than that now. I also plan to talk to her dad again.

I know I am brave, you don't need to tell me.

I manage to get tickets to a local soccer game, and am hoping that my offering will "soothe the savage beast," so to speak.

With nothing left to do in the office, I decide to head to the grocery store and pick up some fixings for dinner. I am by no means a Martha Stewart, but I can cook pretty well for a single guy. My mother was very insistent that I know how to look after myself. She said that a man should be able to do for himself anything that he would ask of a woman.

Makes sense, I suppose.

I wonder what Shay is like in the kitchen?

Does she cook, or bake?

Oh, please let me find out that she bakes! I have a terrible sweet tooth, and can't bake a thing to save my life. My mother is always sending me care packages, but it isn't the same as that fresh-from-the-oven taste. My mouth is actually watering right now, while visions of Shay in nothing but an apron, and bent over my oven, fill my head. My penis nods his approval, and my stomach just rumbled his. I have to stop this train of thought if I am going to be able to walk without certain parts pointing the way.

I am pleased to inform you that my dick is healing just fine. It has been able to get varying degrees of erections, and the rainbow of colors is diminishing more each day. I am hopeful that by this time next week, I can take him for a test drive. Before I allow him to play with others, I will have to see how well he plays alone. I haven't wanted to try any "self-love,' just yet. I am still afraid of damaging him worse. Next Thursday marks my two week hiatus from sex. I have it marked on all the calendars, as if I would forget.

I'm exiting out the back door, with my keys in hand, ready to hit the automatic locks. Just as I open the doors, I become aware that something is very wrong.

The smell of paint is the first thing that tips me off. I clutch my keys tighter as I scan the area. At first I don't see it, because I am looking at the building and surrounding area, but then I do. I let out a roar, as I run over to my vehicle.

The words, "Fuck You," are spray-painted across the one side of my car. It looks fresh too, as the paint is just starting to run. I whip around quickly and scan the area more closely. There is no one around, and no evidence that points to who did this, although I have my suspicions. I pocket my keys, and pull out my phone. I snap some pictures of the vandalism, and then send Dante a text with the pictures attached. He answers immediately, saying that he is on his way, and not to touch anything.

I put my phone back in my pocket and just stare at the offensive words. I can feel my blood pressure rising with each thunderous beat of my heart. I turn away from the sight before I do something stupid, like put my fist through the window. I begin to pace while I am stewing over this. It had to be either Kylie or Trisha that did this. I thought that if I didn't press charges after Trisha grabbed me, the whole mess would go away.

Fuck, was I wrong!

The worst part is, I am the victim in all of this!

After having an epic meltdown, and a few temper tantrums, I hear the sounds of Dante's Harley. I pace back to the car just as he is pulling up. He kills the engine and kicks the stand for the bike down. In the blink of an eye, he is off the bike, with helmet in hand, and storming towards me. The guy can be scary, and I am glad that the anger radiating off him in waves isn't for me. He gives me a tight nod and then proceeds to inspect my vehicle. Once he has made a complete circuit, he comes back to take a closer look at the paint. He bends down and starts scratching at something in the gravel right beside the car. He picks something out of the dirt, and then stands to face me. He is holding what appears to be a fingernail.

Gross!

I take a closer look, and realize that it is actually a fake nail, which is not as bad, but still gross.

"I am hoping that this belongs to the perp, and that there is enough DNA on here to identify them. It is a long shot though, as it could belong to anyone. Do you remember if either of those two twits wore fake nails?" Dante has his eyebrow raised at me and is waiting for an answer.

"Honestly, I wasn't looking at Kylie's hands that night when we were having sex. The other time I saw her, she was molesting me and I didn't notice then either. Trisha, I am pretty sure didn't though. Not sure why I think that, I just do. We can ask Laney about Trisha. She might remember better, seeing as how they rumbled."

Dante sighs, and then looks back at the paint. "We can also see if either of them paid by credit card anytime they were in the club. They would have had to sign the receipt, and then we can possibly match it to the writing on your car. Do me a solid here, my man, and don't mention any of this to the cops when they get here. Just let them file this for your insurance purposes. Blow it off, and make it seem that you have no idea who it might be. I have connections that can get our answers faster without having the cops sticking their noses in and messing everything up while they just stand around with their dicks out."

Dante then turns and heads for his bike. He pops a button, and the back seat opens up to reveal a hidden compartment. He removes what looks like a small baggie, which he then puts the nail into, and returns it to the compartment. He snaps the seat shut, and turns to me with an air of innocence and a look on his face, daring me to say anything.

What the hell?

I don't have a chance to ask him about his connections, or his James Bond bike, as the police are now arriving. I am pretty sure that all of this is off the radar, and possibly illegal, hence why he doesn't want the cops knowing.

What secrets are my friends hiding from me?

☺

After the police take down all the information they need to file their report, I'm free to take my vehicle in for repairs. Dante snaps a few pictures of the evidence, and then gives me the address of a guy he knows who can get the paint off for me. I am really becoming suspicious of my friends and what kinds of skeletons they are hiding in their closets. I write the address down, and agree to let Dante know how it goes. He then puts his helmet on, mounts and starts his bike, releases the stand, and speeds away. I shake my head and decide to worry about what he is hiding at a later time.

My car is unlocked, as the police wanted to do a quick search. So I hop in and head to the address that Dante has given me.

It is in the shadier part of town, and somehow I am not surprised. I pull up to the address, expecting to find a business, but it is just a house. There is a huge garage beside it though that looks like it could hold six cars easily. I put the car in park and shut the engine off.

What now?

Do I just knock on the front door, or do I head towards the garage and hope someone is there?

I am sitting here, deciding what to do, when there is a knock on my window.

Now, given the stress of the day so far, it is not my fault that I screamed like a little girl.

Once I am convinced that my heart did not just leap from my chest, I turn towards the person who scared a year off my life. He is standing on the other side of my door, peering at me through the window. He is of average height and build with blonde spiky hair. He has sunglasses on, so I can't see the color of his eyes. He is wearing faded jeans with dark grease stains and a black wife beater, displaying several tattoos on his arms. I know that he is waiting for me to acknowledge him, but I am still a little shaken. I give myself a mental slap, and open the door to get out of the car. He backs up to let me out, and once I am, he holds his hand out in a gesture for me to give him something. I am slow to realize that he wants my keys, but I am not comfortable just handing them over to someone I don't know and who hasn't even spoken a word to me yet. He must feel my hesitation, so he finally speaks.

"Dante called, and told me you were coming. The name is Trent. I got you covered here. Gimme a few hours and I will have her shining like an apple."

Well, I am still not comfortable with this, but I don't seem to have much choice. I have a few questions first though.

"How long is this going to take and how much is it going to cost me?"

If I seem rude, Trent doesn't notice, or care. "Few hours tops. You can hang in the garage while I work, or you can head home and I will bring it to you when it is done. Your choice."

Actually, I am not happy about either choice. It is one thing to let him work on my car, but another to have him drive it. I also am not feeling like bonding with this guy while he works on my car. "You didn't say how much? Also, how do you know, Dante?"

"No charge, I owe Dante. As for how I know him, if you are asking me that, then he hasn't told you, and I am not going to be the one to tell."

He is standing more defiantly now.

I can take a hint. Time for me to get out of here.

I still feel uneasy about leaving my car with him, but I am sure as hell not staying. "Okay, message received. I am going to call for a cab, and I will hear from you in a few hours then. Let me give you my card."

I pull my wallet out, and hand him one of my business cards. He takes the card, but doesn't bother to look at it. He motions for me to move so he can get in my car. I move to the sidewalk, watch as he starts it, and then backs it towards the ramp for the garage. The door to the garage opens as he is backing the car up. I get a peek inside, and I am quite impressed by what I see. He has a clean and very professional-looking setup inside. Once my car is inside, the door closes and I am alone on the street. Not wasting any time, I whip out my phone and dial for a cab.

Time to escape *The Twilight Zone*.

Bent

Chapter Sixteen

True to his word, Trent calls a few hours later and then delivers my car to me.

I meet him in front of my building. When I try to give him some money, he gets pissed. He might be just an average-looking guy, but I get the feeling that he's more than he seems. Not daring to push my luck, I drop the subject of money. I ask him how he's getting home, and he says he's hooking-up with someone in the area. Not wanting to find out what that entails, I thank him and let him be on his way.

I have to admit, my car is shining like a polished apple. There is no evidence left of the paint. I'm a happy man again. I jump into my car and pull it around to the ramp for the underground parking garage. Once it's parked safely beside my baby, I head back up to my condo.

I never did get to the grocery store, and don't feel like ordering something and eating alone. Once inside and sitting on a stool in my kitchen, I weigh my options.

Logan is probably still wallowing and won't be great company even if he agrees to go out. I desperately want to talk to Dante about everything that happened today, but it can wait. What I really want is to see Shay. I need to let her know that I had made the arrangements for the fishing date anyway, so I can use that as my excuse for wanting to see her.

I take my phone out of my pocket and pull up her number. Hmm...do I text her, or call her? She might busy, so a text would be better.

How is my favorite girl?

I wait several minutes before she replies. I am sitting back down on the stool, after getting a beer from the fridge, when my phone beeps with her message.

Favorite girl, huh? I like the sound of that :-)

I smile, as I text her back.

Good, cuz it's true. I made the arrangements for our next date. Are you free to meet me?

I hold my breath while I await her reply. Good thing she answers quickly or I might have passed out.

A pre-date, date? LOL

If you want to call it that.

Ok. Where and when?

Good question. My usual choices cater mostly to men, being pubs and roadhouses. I try to think of a place that is close to both our homes. I know of a small pizzeria that has amazing food and coffee, and is close to her. Now, should I offer to pick her up, or do we each drive ourselves and meet there? Only one way to find out.

Do you know where Luigi's is?

Yes! I love their pizza.

Perfect. Woman.

Perfect. Do you want to meet, or be picked-up? Say in half an hour?

I will meet you since I am at the magazine office. Cya soon.

Soon.

I place my phone on the counter. I need to change quickly, and primp a bit.

What?

Do you think it's just women who do that? Men are just as vain, we just hide it better.

I head into the bedroom to transform into something that will make her mouth water for *me* as much as the pizza.

☺

I arrive at Luigi's ahead of schedule. I want to make sure that we have a decent table. It is a small establishment, and can get pretty busy. I am in luck though, and manage to get a booth by the window. Once I am seated, I glance outside in time to see Shay exiting her car. My heart skips a beat at the sight of her. I always appreciate curves on a woman instead of bones, and Shay has the best curves ever.

Today she is wearing a black, form-fitting skirt that ends just below her knees. She has this paired with a fitted, red blazer that cinches in at her waist and accentuates her hourglass figure. She has on killer, red heels that do amazing things for her calves which I am picturing wrapped around my neck. I have to adjust myself under the table, and my pants suddenly feel three sizes too small.

Easy, Big Guy. Soon.

She enters the restaurant and scans the tables. I assume that she is looking to see if I am here yet, so I wave at her from where I am sitting. Her whole face lights up when she sees me, and I can feel myself sighing at the sight of that smile. She makes her way towards the table, and slides into the booth across from me.

Now that she is so close to me, her beauty leaves me speechless. She smiles at me again, and I feel my heart skip another beat.

At this rate, I might suffer heart failure.

She takes in my appearance, and I can see her pupils begin to dilate while her lips part slightly.

Oh yes, she is appreciating the primping that I have done.

I left my hair in its usual style, but I am freshly shaved. I am wearing my favorite pair of black jeans, which I have been told shows off my package nicely. I have on a green Henley, which brings out the color in my eyes, with the sleeves pushed up. It seems to be a turn-on for the ladies (something about men's forearms). Shay is definitely looking turned-on.

Score!

She comes out of her Alex-induced trance and smiles sheepishly at me.

"This was a great idea, Alex. I was starving, and about to grab a quick bite on my way home. This is so much better. Thank you for inviting me."

I have to swallow the drool out of my mouth before I can speak. While she was saying all that, she removed her blazer, revealing that underneath she is wearing a low-cut camisole in white. I can see her white lace bra through the material, and I swear that her nipples popped out just for me.

"I'm glad that you could make it. Do you want something to drink before we order? They serve some alcoholic beverages here, as well as the usual refreshments, and an amazing cup of coffee."

"I would love a glass of red wine. It was a hectic day at the office, but very productive. I have quite a good start on my article about harassment in the work place. Thanks again for all that you guys are doing to help me."

"It is nothing. We are glad to help." I flag the waitress over to order Shay her wine, and myself a beer.

The waitress who approaches the table has a bit too much swagger for my liking. Her hair is swaying around her shoulders in a blonde cloud, and her bright blue eyes are lined artfully to appear more vivid. She has a decent rack, and she is staring straight at me with a cat-like smile on her cherry-red lips.

Before Shay, I would have been hitting that. Now, her blatant appreciation just annoys me.

Does she not see that I have a woman with me?

She completely ignores Shay, and leans suggestively towards me. I am getting rather pissed at the obvious display of her boobs in my face, and am about to say something, when Shay intercedes.

"Excuse me, miss? I know that my date is rather pretty, and very easy on the eyes, but show some class and some respect. If this is a problem for you, I am sure that the manager would be willing to accommodate us. With that being said, I would like a red wine, and my date would like something as well."

Holy shit!

That just happened.

Shay has claws!

She just gave a verbal smack down to our sleazy waitress, but with style and intelligence. I think that is the first time a woman has ever risen to my defense, and I liked it!

Our waitress straightens with a snap, and whips out her notepad. She apologizes for her behavior, and promises that it is not necessary to get the manager. She asks me, without making eye contact, what I would like to drink, and then says that she will be back with our drinks and to take our dinner order if we are ready.

She practically runs away from our table, and I am left with my little spitfire.

She looks innocently at me, but I see the sparkle in her eyes that she is trying to hide.

I think it is at this precise moment that I start falling in love with her.

She winks at me, and then casually picks up her menu to look through. I follow suit, but I already know what I want. I always get the same thing when I come here. I ask Shay what she is thinking about ordering, and she asks if we can share a pizza. Perfect, as that is what I always get. We wait until our waitress returns and takes our order for a pizza with pepperoni, mushrooms and green peppers on one half for me, and onions, tomatoes and extra cheese on the other half for Shay.

When she is gone, I rest my arms on the table and decide to tell Shay about my day, leaving out the parts regarding Dante and his secrets. She listens raptly to everything that I tell her. When I am finished, she leans forward and gives voice to thoughts that I have already entertained.

"Do you think that those two bitches are done, or do you believe they might try something else?"

"I was wondering the same thing myself earlier. I can't do anything about it without proof that it was them, but I plan on being extra careful from now on. I would ask that you do the same, Shay. So far they seem to be targeting me, for obvious reasons, but who knows what else they might do, or to whom."

She grabs my hands with her much smaller, and softer ones. She gently starts to stroke my knuckles, easing the tension I hadn't even realized I was holding there.

"Don't worry about me, but I promise to be careful. My dad made sure that I know how to take care of myself, so I am not as fragile as I appear."

Speaking of her father, this reminds me that I have the soccer tickets for him. I may as well run the idea past Shay before I go and make a fool of myself in front of him.

"Speaking of your dad, I found out from Logan that he likes soccer, so I got a couple of tickets to a soccer match. Do you think that he might want to go to a game with me? You know, so he can get to know me a bit better, and I can hopefully gain his approval for dating you."

At this, Shay bursts out laughing.

Umm ... not the reaction I was expecting or hoping for here.

What did I miss?

She finally gets control of herself, but her eyes are still dancing when she answers me.

"I'm sorry, that wasn't very nice. The thing is, no man has ever worried about what my father thinks. I'm not sure how to answer that. I think it is awfully sweet of you to give him the respect of trying to earn his approval. That alone should earn you some points. He is very protective of me, and I don't think he will ever believe that any man is good enough for his 'little girl,' but the right man might change his mind. I really don't know what he would think of the tickets. The only way to know for sure would be to ask. I also think that if you want to win my dad over, the best way is through my mom. He might be a big, tough lawyer to the world, but he is a huge softie around her. She can make that man dance to any tune she wants, so I would go through my mom to reach my father. Are the tickets open, or are they for a specific game date?"

I was smart enough to get open tickets for any game date, because I am sure that her dad is a busy man.

"Open, that way he could choose which game he wanted to see."

Shay smiles, and nods approvingly. "Good. Here is what I suggest then. Their anniversary is this weekend, I mentioned this to you yesterday. I would make a gesture by sending flowers to my mother for their anniversary, she loves fresh flowers, but address the card to both of them. I was planning on taking them out to dinner on Sunday, so have them delivered that afternoon. Trust me on this, she will love it. Hopefully she will bend his ear about how thoughtful it was of you, and he will be more receptive when you decide to ask him to the game. Honestly though, why does it matter so much to you what my father thinks of you, or if he approves?"

What I want to say is, "Because you matter to me," but what I say is, "It is the decent thing to do, when dating his daughter. My mother raised me to have respect for others, and I guess I just want to let him know that I am acknowledging his role as your father."

Shay sighs and closes her eyes, but is smiling. When she opens them, I can see that I said the right thing, and I can feel my chest puffing slightly. Before anything can be said further, our food arrives.

We are both so hungry, that we dive right in. We laugh at each other, as we blow on our slices and try not to make too much of a mess. Between bites of pizza, I tell her about the plans for our fishing date on Monday. I don't tell her about the yacht though, as I want that to be a surprise. She nods around mouthfuls of pizza, and makes sounds of agreement, but polishes off her slice before she speaks. I love to see a woman who enjoys her food. Too many times I have watched women pick at their food, and it drives me nuts.

Eat it already! Half of them could use some extra calories, as they are too thin. Not Shay, though. She eats with relish, and has an amazing figure.

Perfect.

We agree on a time to meet at the dock on Monday, which is nine am, and I tell her to plan on being out the whole day. She asks if she should bring her own fishing gear, or if we are renting. I actually gape at this.

She has her own gear?

She wasn't kidding about her love of fishing!

I can feel myself swooning again.

When the bill comes, I insist on paying. Shay tries to argue that she can pay her own half, but I refuse. I tell her I am paying because I invited her out. We agree that she can leave the tip, which if it were up to me would have been nothing. But Shay is classy, and leaves one anyway.

I escort her out to her car, and don't even wait until we are there, before I spin her around and gently take her face between my hands, bending down to press my lips to hers.

I could not have waited a moment more.

Her plump lips have tempted me all through our meal. I was forced to watch them sipping from her wine glass, parting for her food, her tongue licking them clean whenever she took a bite of her pizza.

I was, of course, visualizing her licking something else clean.

A man can only take so much, and thank God the table was covering my reaction to all the lip porn!

Shay gives as good as she gets, and damned if that doesn't turn me on more. Her aggressive response to my kiss delivers waves of arousal up and down my spine. I can taste the tartness of the wine and the spices from the pizza sauce on her lips and tongue, but underneath all that is the taste of Shay. I could stand here and kiss her all night, and I know if I don't end this soon, that I will be fondling her in seconds. I begin to gentle the kiss, pulling back slowly from her. Her eyes are still shut, and I bend to kiss each of her lids. Then I bring her head close to my chest and just hold her in my arms, and nothing has ever felt so right. She snuggles in and wraps her arms around me. I press a kiss to the top of her head, and tell her how much I wish tomorrow was Monday. She nods her head against me and murmurs her agreement. I remind her that we still get to see each other at work, and promise to try and find a way for us to navigate the mire of Logan's rules regarding dating in the workplace so we can spend time together there as well.

Reluctantly, we ease apart and I walk her the last few feet to her car. I bend, give her a gentle kiss on the lips, and then help her into her car. I stand back and watch as she backs up, and then she turns around and drives away.

I am still standing there, watching her tail lights, when I feel someone approaching. On instant alert, I spin around and scare the poor woman who is walking to her car. I apologize to her and explain that I was startled. She politely nods her head, but she is still looking at me like I might jump her at any second. I walk over the few spots to where my car is parked, unlock the doors, and hop in.

    I need to get home and see what Dante may have found out. I start the car, and drive away.

Chapter Seventeen

When I get home, I contact Dante right away. I am not too surprised that I don't get an answer when I call him. He does send me a text back, saying that he can't answer his phone, but he has information for me. He says he will meet with me tomorrow for coffee. I text back that I will meet him for ten at our usual coffee shop around the corner from the club. He replies that he will see me then. Dante has always been more reclusive than Logan or I, but the Cloak and Dagger is making me feel uneasy.

What is going on with my friends?

I feel like I haven't really known them these past eleven years. I decide to put these thoughts to rest for the night.

I head through to my bedroom, change out of the clothes that I wore to meet with Shay and into some workout clothes. I have a routine at night that I do to keep in shape besides hitting the gym three times a week. I haven't been going to the gym this last week because of my injury, but I have still been doing my own stretching and toning at home. I do sit-ups and pushups on the floor, along with a few other exercises.

I am going through my routine, but my mind is on Shay. I am obviously extremely attracted to her physically, but it is more than that. I am equally attracted to her mind and her vibrant personality. I can honestly say that I have never felt this way before. As my mind is distracted with thoughts of Shay, my penis reacts to these thoughts as well. I am having trouble continuing my exercises with a kickstand in my way. I stop the crunches that I am doing, and just lay there on my back, allowing my mind to wander, since it wants to anyway. A graphic display of all her physical attributes take a decidedly pornographic turn. The killer-red heels are having a starring role, since they are the only thing that my mind has allowed to remain on her body. She is crawling on all fours towards me in my mind, her generous, creamy breasts are swaying seductively while she is licking her plump lips. Her eyes are telling me all the wicked things that she is going to allow me to do to her. My penis is throbbing in my shorts and my balls are starting to ache.

I groan, and allow my hand to slide down inside my shorts, to grasp my straining erection. I suck in a huge gulp of air at the tingles that shoot out from my dick to travel up my spine and around my balls. I have missed this so much, and if it is going to happen, I am not going to last long. I give myself a nice long stroke, and my eyes roll back in my head.

Oh God, that felt good.

There is a constant stream of pre-cum leaking from the tip, so I rub some of it around the head and down my length for lubrication. I am panting and biting my lip by the time I am finished doing this.

Time to get serious with the self-pleasuring.

With a firm grip on The Big Guy and with visions of Shay dancing before my eyes, I begin to pump. My hips shoot up and off the floor from the overwhelming sensations. I quickly jerk my shorts down and out of the way with my free hand so that I can give myself more room, and begin to massage my balls as well. I moan while thrusting my hips into my hand and I can't remember a jerk ever feeling this good. I am picking up speed, and the friction is just what I need. With one final thrust, I shout out Shay's name, and go off with so much force I believe I might have hit the ceiling.

Holy Fuck!

That was one of the best orgasms of my life, and I haven't even gotten inside her yet!

I am still going, but with less force. I am panting and covered in sweat and other fluids, yet I have never felt so alive.

I decide to look down to see how my penis is doing after that, since technically I wasn't supposed to masturbate yet. I swear it is waving at me, and looking quite smug, but still a little discolored. I flop my head back down, and make a silent promise to be gentle with him, just in case.

The next time he is allowed out to play will be with Shay.

I am waiting at the coffee shop for Dante. It is a few minutes before ten, so I go ahead and order our coffee. I always get cream in mine, but Dante drinks his black. I don't know how he can drink it that way. I tried it black once, but I couldn't get more than a sip past my lips. It was too strong and bitter. I take our cups over to a table in the back where there are no other patrons. I am not sure what Dante has to tell me, but I'm sure that it isn't information that we want overheard.

I am just placing our drinks down, when I see him approaching.

He is dressed all in black, with a black leather jacket. I don't know why I haven't noticed before, but he seems to always be dressed in black. I guess I always assumed that he just liked the color, but now I am thinking there are other reasons. His shoulder-length hair is loose today and not tied back per his usual.

He sits at the table and removes his sunglasses. His brown eyes are bloodshot, and he looks like he hasn't had much sleep. I hope that I am not the cause of this, even indirectly. I take my seat across from him and wait for him to speak. He doesn't waste any time and gets straight to the point.

"It was them. I didn't have to dig too far to find the information. Seems that they are pretty dumb and posted all about it on Facebook. They didn't name you, but they did brag about how they got revenge on, and I quote here, "Penis Freak" and his car. You sure know how to pick them, my man." He smirks, and then reaches for his cup.

Penis Freak?

I feel steam coming out of my ears. "Technically, I only picked one of them. What am I supposed to do now, tell the police?"

Dante finishes his gulp of coffee, and places it back on the table. "No, let me handle it. I have someone watching them. If they make another move against you, I will know and be able to stop them. I'm sure that I can scare them better than the police ever could. They won't be bothering you again," he says this rather ominously.

I just stare at him openly now.

What is Dante into that he has "someone" watching them and that he can "scare" them?

"Thank you for dealing with all of this for me." He inclines his head towards me, in acknowledgement of my thanks. "But how are you going to make all this happen?"

"The less you know, the better. Let me just say this, because I can tell by the look on your face that you are not going to let it drop, the club isn't the only job I have these days. I am not part of anything illegal, and nothing I do will come back on the club."

WTF?

I knew something else was going on!

There are a million questions that I want to ask, but I can tell by looking at the rigid set to Dante's features, that I would be wasting my breath. I have one thing that I want to say to him though.

"We have been friends for a long time now. I trust you with my life, and I hope that you feel the same way. If you cannot tell me what you are into now, that is fine. You will tell me at some point though, right?"

Dante pinches the bridge of his nose, and closes his eyes while he answers. "Yes, but not right now. There are things happening that are preventing me from sharing, with anyone. But once the shit has been cleared, I will tell you and Logan. I owe you both that much."

Well that was vague, and even more suspicious, but at least he has agreed to tell us.

He has released his nose and opened his eyes. He is staring at me and waiting for me to accept what he has just said. I nod my head and lift my cup for a much needed drink of coffee.

Dante is smirking again, and I know the subject is about to be changed.

"Do you have any plans to see Shay soon? Or her dad?"

Asshole.

"Actually, I met her last night for dinner to discuss our next date. Get this, she wants to go fishing. She has her own fishing gear and everything."

Dante's eyebrows shoot up in surprise. "Really? I shouldn't be too surprised. She was a tomboy growing up, and her dad's only child. He happens to be an excellent fisherman."

"How do you know all this?"

"I have done some computer and security work for her dad. He has fishing trophies in his office, and we got talking about it one day. He didn't mention Shay being into fishing though."

I feel a pang of jealousy that Dante appears to get along with her dad when her dad seems like he would rather chop off my balls than have a conversation with me. I also fear I may be a bit envious of him having information on Shay that I don't.

"How did you know that she was a tomboy?"

Dante chuckles at this. "We all remember what she was like as a kid. She was what, thirteen when we met Logan?" At my nod, he continues. "Her dad also has pictures in his office of her over the years. She wasn't turning the boy's heads back then, so I guess she fit in better as one of them. She played all kinds of sports according to her father, and her pictures and trophies are in his office. He mentioned how she was always a tough kid when she was little. She climbed trees, played with bugs, and wasn't afraid of anything."

I can so easily picture a young Shay, just like Dante is describing. She is still fearless, and I can always give her something to play with and then climb, if you get my meaning.

"Well, I can actually picture her that way. She is still fearless."

I tell Dante about the incident with the waitress. After we have a good chuckle over how well Shay handled her, Dante sobers and looks me straight in the eye.

"She is a great catch, and I am happy for you. Don't blow it."

I know he doesn't mean to hurt me, but he does. Why does everyone assume that I am going to do something to hurt her or screw up my chances with her?

"I am not going to blow anything!" Okay, that didn't sound right. "I really like her, and know what an amazing woman she is, and trust me I know how lucky I am. Please, just have faith in me for once. I am not going to screw this up."

"Sorry, man. I didn't mean it that way. I just see how happy you are right now, and I don't want anything to change that. Some of us can only wish for that." He averts his eyes when he says this last part. I have a feeling he is referring to himself, and confirms for me that he at least wants more from a woman, unlike Logan. I clear my throat to get his attention.

"Look, I wasn't looking for it to happen. It will happen for you too, when you least expect it."

His cheeks color slightly. I decide to spare us both from this awkward, "girly" moment.

"Hey, I have to go over to the club. Want to come with me, and go over the plans for this weekend's theme?"

He gives me a relieved look, and says that he will meet me there.

Bring on the weekend!

Chapter Eighteen

The rest of that day and night are pretty uneventful, so I will skip ahead to where things start to get interesting again.

It is now Saturday night, and we have just opened the doors. There is a steady line of customers, and quite a large crowd outside. This week's theme is, "Jamaica." There is lush Jamaican scenery on the walls, and Bob Marley is singing through the speaker system. We have a band setting up to start playing in the next hour. They have played for us before, and they are really good. They are going to play a variety of Island music. The smells of bananas, coconuts and exotic flowers swirl in the air, and there is a breeze moving through the club as well. The staff are wearing sarongs and shirts, in the colors of the Jamaican flag. Our bar is serving authentic Jamaican Rum Punch and Red Stripe Beer. We have a Jamaican snack menu as well. It all feels very real, and I can say this with honestly as I have been to Jamaica.

Actually, all three of us went just after college graduation. It was a blur of beer and boobs, hard-ons and hook-ups, but I do remember some of it and the Island itself.

Good times!

I am making my rounds, when I notice a rather large group of girls eyeing me from a table by the bar. Actually, they appear to be eyeing my crotch. I panic, thinking my fly is down, or that I have a boner I am unaware of, but when I look down, I see nothing is going on. Maybe these pants draw attention to my package?

I am wearing a pair of Diesel jeans in a light wash that are fitted but not painted on.

By the way, I have great legs that are long and muscular. My ass is pretty impressive too, and my package speaks for itself, but doesn't appear to be speaking too loudly right now, not enough to garner this much attention anyway. If they don't stop staring, they are going to see more than I want them too.

Hey, I am a guy!

If my dick is getting this much attention, it is going to preen.

Just a fact.

I turn around and head off in another direction. Pretty soon, the girls and their cock-hungry eyes are forgotten. My eyes land on the object of my desire. She is serving her first table of the night.

We have managed to keep her patrons limited to mostly females, and so far things have gone well for her, and for us.

She is leaning over the table to hear the orders that are being shouted at her, and I let out a little whimper. The sarong is wrapped around her breasts, and displaying them to the table like ripe melons. There is a tease of cleavage, and I find myself straining to see better, and hoping for a wardrobe malfunction. Just a little one, to show me more of her bountiful bosom.

On second thought maybe not, as I wouldn't be the only one with a peek and there is one guy at the table that is staring at her boobs, like the answers to the universe are hidden there. She is smiling and oblivious to all the dirty thoughts that are aimed at her chest. She straightens and sashays over to the bar to place her table's order. The boob-guy leans over and whispers something to his buddy, who nods his head in agreement to whatever has been said. I know I should let it go, but I am alpha enough that I cannot allow another to sniff around what I consider is mine.

I walk briskly over to the table. I don't announce my presence, but then I never really have to. The girls at the table all start to murmur to each other, and have their eyes glued to me. I hear them saying things like, "He's hot," "Omigod, I want him," and "I want to have his babies." These are all things that I have heard before, but the two guys at the table obviously haven't. They turn their heads to see what the girls are talking about. When the one who was eyeing, Shay makes eye contact with me, I make sure that my face is showing my displeasure. He looks a little confused about this. I clarify things for him.

"Good evening, ladies. My name is Alex, and I am one of the owners of the club. Please excuse me while I address your male companions for the night." At this, I make sure that I am glaring at the Boob Ogler. "Our staff works very hard here to make sure that you are well taken care of. They deserve your respect, and consideration. I realize that some of our staff is especially pleasing on the eyes and looking is natural, but I do not want anyone made to feel uncomfortable, due to obscene staring at their body parts. I am sure that you can understand how that would make for an unpleasant working experience?"

The guy has the grace to look embarrassed. He nods his head vigorously and so does his friend. Pleased at how well this went, I smile to take the sting out of it. After all, they are just kids and paying customers. I thank them for their understanding of the matter. The girls at the table are alternating their looks between death glares at the two guys and hopeful smiles towards me. I give each of them a coupon for a free drink to use throughout the evening. The girls all squeal and the guys look at me with respect now.

Yeah, I figured that would smooth things over.

I retreat from the table before Shay returns, and I resume my rounds throughout the club.

I feel eyes on me, and turn to see where it is coming from. The Crotch Groupies by the bar are staring at me again. I am starting to get a bad feeling, and lately all my bad feelings have been right. I decide to head over to security and talk to Dante about it.

He isn't at his usual post by the door, so I decide to peek into the office.

The door is shut, and it appears the lights are off inside. Still, I open the door anyways, and flick on the lights.

I could never have anticipated what I would walk in on.

My eyes will never be able to un-see the scene before me.

Dante is sitting in one of the chairs with his pants around his knees. On his lap, is a writhing woman, with her top open and her skirt wrapped around her waist high enough so I can clearly see that she waxes.

Dante has one hand wrapped around her hair, and the other is squeezing a boob, while he impales her on his massive cock. He doesn't even stop what he is doing, and the woman seems too far gone to care.

I blink, hoping that I am not seeing this.

Dante has his eyes clenched shut, and is gritting his teeth in obvious pleasure, but still manages to speak.

"You can leave now. Lock the door when you go."

I don't have to be told twice!

I beat a hasty retreat, turning out the lights, and shutting and locking the door behind me. I am standing on the other side of the door now, with no clue how to process what I just witnessed.

Dante, NEVER screws around while he is working. I may have a time or two, and I know Logan has used his office during business hours for more than crunching numbers, but I was pretty sure that Dante had never crossed that line.

Guess I was wrong.

One of the security staff notices me standing there and approaches. He doesn't look happy.

"Is Dante done questioning that chick yet? We need to start rotation, and he has the schedule."

Umm ... questioning her? Unless the answer was in her crotch, I am pretty sure he wasn't questioning her.

I shake my head in the negative because I don't know what else to say. The guy just grunts, and then walks away. Guess that was answer enough.

I finally peel myself away from the door and I walk in a daze towards the bar. I don't even pay attention to the table of woman who have been staring at me. I walk to the end of the bar and flag Laney over. If anyone has the dirt about anything that goes on in the club, it is her. She must know that something isn't right by the look on my face, for she rushes over to me.

Laney really is a stunning woman. She has the most amazing shade of auburn hair, which falls in a gleaming curtain down to her perfectly shaped ass. Her eyes are an unusual shade of gold, but that only adds to her allure. She has a tall and slender build, but has nice round hips, and breasts that are full and firm.

Yes, I have noticed her boobs.

I am a guy, and our eyes are drawn to a pair of breasts, naturally. She also has the most adorable dimples. Like I said, stunning.

"What can I do for you, Alex?" She leans against the bar as she waits to hear why I have called her over.

How do I ask this without sounding like a giant asshole? Might as well just spit it out.

"Have you ever noticed if Dante has gotten with a woman, while we are open?"

She raises both eyebrows at me and her mouth falls slightly open.

Yep, it sounded just as bad as I thought it would.

She recovers fast enough though. "You mean in a sexual manner?"

"Yes, that is what I mean."

This is awkward. I shift on my feet as she gives me a curious look.

"Actually, there was one time last month when I overheard the security guys gossiping about him. They were going on about how he took a girl into the office and apparently she was having trouble walking when she left." She raises her one eyebrow at me, questioningly.

I am not going to discuss Dante's "Pet Monster" with her.

Yes, that is his dick's nickname. If you think that is bad, wait until you find out what Logan's is called.

She realizes that I am not going to confirm or deny anything, so she continues, "I can't say for sure though, as I have never seen him with a woman, even outside of office hours."

"Thanks, Laney. I will have to ask him about it."

She starts to look panicked. "He isn't going to get in trouble is he? I wouldn't have said anything, and it is just gossip anyways."

I smile at her loyalty. I hope Logan gets his head out of his ass and sees what is right under his nose. She is a treasure.

"He isn't in trouble, relax. I was just asking because I may have just walked in on him with a woman, in the security office."

She gasps, and her hands fly up to her mouth to cover reaction. Her eyes are bugging out, and I decide to calm her reaction fast.

"It isn't a big deal. I was just a bit shocked to see him doing that when he is so rigid about how security is run. Please don't say anything to anyone, especially Logan."

At the mention of Logan's name, a cloud passes over her face.

"You don't have to worry about me saying anything, especially to Logan. He is avoiding me."

Logan, needs his ass kicked!

"I know I can trust you, Laney. Don't worry about, Logan. I think he was dropped on his head too many times as a baby." This gives her the giggle I was hoping for.

"Well, if there isn't anything else, I need to get back to my tables. I will see you later, Alex."

"Thanks, Laney."

I watch as she walks back to the area that she serves. Several pairs of appreciative male eyes follow her progress as well. Logan is a fool. When he finally figures his shit out, it may be too late.

Well, now that I have this information about Dante, I am not sure what to do with it. I am guilty of sampling the goods at work myself, I just didn't imagine him doing the same. Actually, I don't have to imagine it, because it is burnt into my retinas!

Ugh, how am I ever going to scrub those images from my mind? Seeing one of my friends playing "Hide the Salami" is not something that I ever wanted to witness.

I need a drink, but that is against Logan's rules.

Fuck it!

Seems like rules are being broken around here a lot lately, so I may as well as add another to the list.

I signal one of the bartenders over and order a double scotch, neat. I turn around to survey the club as I wait. The group of Package Peepers is at it again. They are not being as discreet now either, probably due to the alcohol they have been consuming. Two of them are actually pointing at my groin and giggling.

What the hell is going on here?

I am getting a very bad feeling now.

I feel a tap on my arm, and turn around expecting to find the bartender with my drink. There is a woman standing there instead, and she seems vaguely familiar. It finally clicks that this is the chick that Dante was boning

I didn't recognize her with her clothes on.

"You don't know me, but my friends and I came here tonight to cause some trouble for you. Your friend has shown me that this would be a bad idea, and I am apologizing to you for that." She won't look me in the eyes as she speaks. Well, it appears that Dante was doing more than just showing her his Monster.

What the hell is going on?

They were going to cause trouble for me?

How?

Why?

My questions are quickly answered.

"You see, we are friends of Kylie's. She wanted us to make every woman here aware of your 'problem.' I am so sorry. We only heard her side of the story, and it is pretty bad. We just wanted to protect our friend. We had no idea that she was lying. Your friend could have thrown us all out, but he made me promise to finish our drinks, and leave without a scene. We won't be bothering you. I really am sorry."

I shouldn't be shocked by anything that involves Kylie, The Crotch Killer, but I am. I am starting to hear the theme to *Psycho* in my head every time her name is mentioned.

Time to find Dante and find out what else happened in that room, besides what my eyes refuse to forget!

Chapter Nineteen

After my drink arrives, I down it, and head back in the direction of the office which is by the front door.

Dante isn't by the door, so I find myself in front of the office again. I am reluctant to enter though, so I decide to knock first this time. Dante shouts for me to come in. I hesitantly open the door, and slowly peek my head inside. Dante is on his cell, leaning against the back wall. He says something into his phone, and then ends the call. He nods for me to come in. I edge around the door, and shut it behind me. We stand there staring at each other. The chair that was being used the last time I was in here, is pushed back under the desk. I find my eyes drawn to it, as if it will have all the answers. I hear Dante sigh, and look back to him, quickly noticing that he looks constipated.

Well, at least this seems to be as uncomfortable for him as it is for me.

"Look, I don't want to talk about what you may, or may not, have seen. The only thing I am willing to discuss is the reason behind it." He walks over to the desk and pulls out the chair. "You may want to sit for this."

Excuse me?

I am not sitting on that chair after what I saw going on in it! The chair could have been used for more than what I witnessed, and I feel a shiver work its way up my spine at the thought of what could be on that chair. When I don't move, Dante realizes why.

"Oh for fuck's sake, I cleaned it. Don't be a pussy!" He points to the chair as he says this.

All the same, I think I will stay standing. "Just tell me what it is that I need to hear."

"Fine, suit yourself. I noticed the way those girls were acting when they arrived here, and the fact that one of them asked a server where Alex Bradley was, tipped me off that something wasn't right. I decided to approach the group myself. It became obvious that no one was going to talk, but one looked like she could be persuaded by the looks she was giving me. I asked her to come with me to the office so that I could give her my number, which was just an excuse to get her to follow me without raising any suspicions. I told the guys that I was just questioning her about something and didn't elaborate. She proved to be more stubborn than I liked. She offered an exchange for her information, so I took it. It's amazing the things that a woman will reveal in the throes of ecstasy. I found out more than she would have revealed otherwise. It appears that Kylie is determined to ruin you. She had asked her friends to come here with the purpose of ruining your reputation with the ladies, and to embarrass you tonight. She has also got an older cousin who could be a problem. Apparently this cousin is part of a gang, and they have been given a crap story from her about you, and they are looking to seek revenge for her." He is giving me hard eyes, and I know that this is way more serious than I thought. "I know of the gang, and have already started the process of finding out what they have planned. I wasn't aware of her gang ties, or just how unstable she seems. I am sorry. I should have looked into this further. I just thought she was a flake, and if I had someone shadowing her, we would have stopped her before she tried anything. I thought that she would just give-up, but that doesn't appear to be happening anytime soon. I think that you should consider going out of town, until I can sort this out."

Okay, now he is starting to scare me. I can tell he knows more than he is telling me, and that he is worried.

"Just what do you think is going to happen? Leaving town seems a bit extreme, don't you think? Also, just how the hell do you think you are going to fix this?"

He pinches the bridge of his nose. "This gang is a pretty bad one, and I don't know how long it is going to take to defuse the situation. I don't want to take any unnecessary risks, plus with you at the club, that makes the club a target as well. I would tell you to just stay away from the club, but we don't know how much information they have, including your address."

My heart is in my throat now. "Jesus, you think it is that bad? How do you know all this, and how are you going to stop them? I should be contacting the cops!"

His eyes snap to mine. "No. This is all circumstantial at best, and the cops won't do anything, but someone might find out that you went to the cops, and that would make things worse."

"How do you know? Dante, what the fuck are you into that you know this shit? Don't you dare say that you can't tell me! I think that I have a right to know, since this concerns me."

He glares at me for a few moments, then just drops his head forward and seems to be bracing himself for whatever it is he is going to tell me. He looks back up at me, and I don't like the look on his face.

"I can't tell you too much right now, but I can tell you that I have been doing some under-cover work for a buddy of mine. I have been doing this for a few years now, and most of the work involves gathering information. Sometimes I have to move in certain circles to get it. This is how I know about the gang that is now targeting you, and I also know certain information that I am sure they will be willing to drop this vendetta for. I can't say any more at this time because of a case that I am working on right now. But trust me that I know what I am doing, and that I would never do anything to jeopardize our friendship or the club."

I do trust him, and I have the utmost faith in him and his abilities. The problem is that what he just told me only makes me more concerned about what he is involved in. It sounds dubious at best, and illegal at worst.

How did we not see any signs that he has been living a double-life? We all have lives outside of each other and the club, but you would think that we would have seen a glimpse of this, only there has been nothing. Either we are extremely ignorant, or he is that good at hiding things from us. I take a really good look at my friend. On the surface, he appears the same as he always does, but if you look deeper, you can see subtle clues that his life isn't all happiness and hard-ons, like I assumed. There are stress lines around his eyes and mouth that I hadn't noticed before. His eyes don't have the same mischievous twinkle they usually do, but instead have a very hard and serious edge to them.

Am I so self-absorbed that I didn't notice these signs before now, or did he hide them well?

"Look, I am not running away. My life is here. I agree that I should avoid making myself an easy target, but I refuse to hide. I can limit my time at the club, and avoid being alone in public."

Dante isn't happy about this, so yes, he looks constipated.

He turns around and starts to pace, while pinching the bridge of his nose. "I will have to put someone on you, to watch out for anything happening. I am setting up a meeting with the cousin, hopefully for tomorrow or Monday. You need to understand, there is no guarantee that the situation will be resolved quickly. There is also another factor that I haven't mentioned." Here, he turns and gives me his most serious eyes. "They could find out about your involvement with Shay, and then she also becomes a target to get to you."

I feel all the blood drain from my face, and my breath freezes in my lungs.

Not, Shay!

I cannot believe that I didn't think of her in all of this. Sure, I warned her about Kylie, but this is different. My sweet, innocent Shay. How am I going to protect her from this? Dante must see the panic on my face.

"She will be protected, calm down. The best way to do this though, is to remove the two of you from the danger. Do you see now why I said you should leave town?"

I am starting to now. "How do I get her to agree to leave with me? She has a job, and her family. She is taking her parents out for their anniversary tomorrow, and we have a fishing date on Monday. How do I ask her to cancel all those things, and just take a leave from her job? What do I tell her? I can't do that to her, I can't!"

I am freaking...the-fuck...out!

I pull out the "sex-chair", and fall into it. At this point, pubes and bodily fluids are the last things on my mind.

I am breathing fast, and feeling a little faint. I lean over, with my elbows on my knees, and cradle my head in my hands.

What a mess!

How could it have gotten so out of hand?

It was supposed to be a night of care-free sex, and it has turned into a nightmare! First my cock gets crunched...twice, then my car is violated, a posse of girls is bent on my destruction, and now a gang is threatening my very life!

Dante's cell phone rings and breaks my internal rant. He pulls it from his pocket, and puts it to his ear. He listens to whatever is being said on the other end and responds with a few grunts. He then tells whoever is on the line to, "Do it." He ends the call and puts his phone away.

"That was my guy who has an 'in' with the gang. He delivered my message, and the cousin has agreed to halt any plans they have on you until I meet with him. The meeting is set-up for Tuesday. You should be safe from them for now. I would still feel better if you could convince Shay to go away with you. I understand that she needs to be with her family tomorrow, but is there a way that you can convince her to turn this fishing date into an overnight? That way, I can focus on the meeting Tuesday without worrying about the two of you. Hopefully, by the end of the day on Tuesday, this will all be over."

"I can try, but do you think it will be that easy?"

The look that comes over Dante is nothing short of, deadly. "He will agree. He will also agree to take care of Kylie, or he won't like the consequences." He practically growls this last part.

I am inclined to believe Dante. I have never seen him look this murderous. Frankly, it scares me.

"Alright, I will ask her tonight and make the arrangements. I am sure that I can keep the boat for another day."

"Make it happen, and let me know when you have everything in place. I am going to make a few more calls, but I need to be alone for these. Go and talk to Shay. You can get women to do anything you want. This shouldn't be too hard for you." He smirks at me.

Bastard.

I nod my head and then stand to leave. I know he just said that last part to lighten the somber mood in here, and I appreciate it, but I don't feel good about any of this.

What have my penis and I gotten everyone into?

Chapter Twenty

Convincing Shay is surprisingly easy. She seems excited at the idea of spending the night with me. I let Dante know that it is a go, and he reassures me that I'm doing the right thing and that he would handle the rest. I'm still not happy with the thought of his meeting with a known gang leader and doing God knows what to convince him to leave me alone and "take care" of his cousin. I don't know if I'm more scared *for* him, or *of* him. Dante has always had a rebellious and dangerous nature, but I never entertained thoughts of him doing anything like this.

Is he a hit man, hired muscle, a goon or a thug?

He is being so vague about this part of his life, and the fact that he has been keeping it from us raises all kinds of flags. I wish I could talk to Logan about it, but I promised Dante that I would keep it to myself until he tells Logan himself.

It is now Sunday, and I have just finished ordering the flowers for Shay's parents' anniversary. Shay said to have them delivered in the afternoon, so I am having them sent to her house for around 3:00pm. She is taking her parents out for dinner at five, so that leaves plenty of time for her mother to wax poetic to her father about my grand gesture. I sure hope this works. I am not looking forward to spending a day with her father given the way he currently feels about me. I put that disturbing thought from my mind, and decide to send Logan a text, letting him know about the overnight with Shay. I grab my phone off the table beside my couch and sit down to text him.

> **I am taking Shay fishing on Monday … we are also staying the night on the yacht I am renting.**

I am holding my breath, waiting for the explosion that is sure to come from Logan. His reply is immediate, but not what I was expecting.

Have fun

That's it?

Granted, I am relieved that he doesn't seem upset by this, but that doesn't seem like Logan. I text back.

R U OK?

Sure

Okay, now I know he isn't fine. He would have had a snappy comeback or just called me a pussy for asking. I decide to just call him instead. The phone doesn't even ring a full two times, before he answers.

"Hey." He sounds like shit!

"What's wrong?" No point wasting words.

"Just a little hung over, I guess."

Wait a minute!

He promised not to do this again, and he rarely drinks these days. Something is very wrong here.

"How much did you drink?"

There is a long pause on his end before he answers. "I don't remember."

"How can you not remember? Logan, where were you drinking? Were you alone again?"

"I started in the office just before we closed. I took a bottle with me to the loft ... I wasn't alone."

Oh no!

What has he done now?

"Okay, you drank a bottle, and you were not alone. Care to elaborate?"

"It was more than a bottle, and no."

Well, fuck that!

He is going to have to tell me more than that. "Who was with you?"

Another long pause. "I don't remember, but I am pretty sure there was more than one person."

"If you don't stop being so vague, I am coming down there!"

"Fuck! Stop yelling in my ear! My head feels like there are ice picks trying to claw their way out. Your voice is getting them excited, and they are clawing faster."

That sounds a bit more like the guy I know. I have two choices here. I either let him go to deal with his hangover, or I let him go and head over there to find out what the hell happened last night.

Yeah, I am going with option two.

"Okay, you go and rest your pretty little head. I will talk to you later."

He lets out a relieved sigh. "Thanks, man. I will text you later." With that, he hangs up.

Oh, he will be talking to me alright, but not via text and not that much later, as I am now grabbing my keys and heading out the door.

☺

I arrive at the club twenty minutes later. After parking my SUV, I decide to head into the office first to see if there are any clues as to why Logan went on a binge again. I have my suspicions. It must have had something to do with Laney. She has been the common factor in all these binges of his lately. I see an empty whiskey glass on the desk, and a few papers neatly stacked off to the side, but otherwise the desk holds no answers. I quickly scan around the room, and that is when I see an image frozen on one of the monitors.

Oh boy!

I can clearly see what has sent him over the edge.

There on the screen is the image of Laney in the passionate embrace of a pretty impressive looking guy. The guy must be at least as muscled as Dante. He appears to be rather tall and has jet black hair from what I can see of him. Laney is wrapped securely in his arms, and looks to be quite happy there. The screen is frozen with the image of their mouths inches apart from each other. It doesn't take a genius to figure out what was coming next. I want to feel bad for Logan but he has done this to himself. If he would only have given her some inclination of what he is feeling for her, I am positive she would wait for him to figure his shit out.

Might as well go and see the extent of the damage that he has done to himself this time. I turn around and exit the office. As I am heading up the stairs leading to the loft, I have to wonder what I may walk in on.

I give him the courtesy of a knock to let him know he is about to have company. I hear movement on the other side, and then the door is yanked open.

He is scowling at me.

Yeah, I figured he wouldn't be happy about my surprise visit, but too bad.

He is wearing his boxers, thankfully, and his hair is rumpled. He doesn't look as bad as he did last time I found him hung-over, but he doesn't look too good either.

He storms away from the door, and I follow, shutting the door behind me. He heads straight for the couch and flops down onto it. He is still scowling, so I decide to take the chair furthest from him. I don't bother easing into this gently.

"I was worried about you, so I decided to see for myself what shape you were in. I also stopped in the office, and saw the video footage on the monitor."

He stops scowling, and just gives me tired eyes instead. He shrugs his shoulder and says, "It was going to happen at some point, even you said as much."

I can tell that he is hurting, so I decide to gentle my approach. "She is a beautiful woman. Men drool over her all the time. You had to know that someone would snatch her up if you didn't."

"I know, I just wasn't prepared for it to hurt so much."

Bingo!

Now we are getting somewhere. "Why don't you just tell her how you feel?"

He turns his head and stares off into space while he answers. "She has the power to make me vulnerable and to hurt me. I won't put myself through that again."

Again?

What am I missing here?

"What do you mean, again?"

"It was a long time ago, but the damage is still there. I won't allow someone to have that kind of power over me. A fuck is all I can offer, and all I am willing to do. Laney would be more than a fuck ... she could be everything. I just can't go there right now with a woman, if ever."

I am beginning to see a bigger picture here, and it is not a happy one.

I had no idea that he was carrying such emotional scars. I am not going to push for answers now, but one day we will be having a talk about all the skeletons that everyone around me seems to have hiding in their closets.

"You can't just ignore the way that you feel about her, though. Look how well that is working out for you."

"I know, but it is the only option for me right now. She deserves to be happy. I can't ask her to wait for me, now can I?"

I am pretty sure he could, and she would. How to say that though?

"Why don't you let her decide what she would do?"

He laughs, but there is no real humor in it. "Sure, I can just see how well that would play out. 'Hey, Laney. I am attracted to you, but I am unwilling to act on it. How about you wait for me anyways, and not date anyone in the meantime?' She would either laugh her ass off, or slap me."

Moron!

"I am sure that you could do better than that. Plus, I think that she might surprise you."

At this, he perks up and looks almost hopeful. "What makes you say that?"

Here goes nothing. "I happen to believe that your feelings are reciprocated. I am not the only one who thinks this either. Also, I know that you are hurting her right now by avoiding her."

His cheeks color slightly.

Yes, I thought that would hit him where it counts. He gets up off the couch and begins to pace while he talks.

"Let's say that you are right, what about what I saw last night?"

"Given the way that you have been treating her, I believe that she was looking for a way to ease the hurt that you are causing her. I don't think that you have anything to worry about there. Besides, you are every woman's wet dream! That guy wouldn't stand a chance against you."

He stops his pacing to look at me, and it is not a happy look. "Well, she isn't the only one who was looking to ease the hurt last night."

This doesn't sound good. "What did you do?"

"I believe, that I brought two women up here last night, it is all really hazy. There might have been more. When I woke up this morning, I was hoping that I didn't have sex with them, but by the amount of empty condom wrappers around the bed, I can assume that I did ... several times."

Wow! And this is why he is a god!

"Well, Laney knows that you are not a saint, and I am pretty sure she knows that you are not celibate, so I don't see how this is a huge problem. As long as you promise to stop banging other chicks while you figure your shit out, she shouldn't be too upset about it."

He just raises his eyebrow at me.

Okay, she might be upset about his having a threesome, or more, being brought to her attention. Too late now, though. I am sure that altars to his prowess are even now being erected around the city in secret female circles. Word about this will make it back to the club, it always does. His only choice is to come clean with her about it and explain that he was a mess over what he saw going down with her.

I tell him this, and even though he looks doubtful, he agrees to talk to her.

Finally!

Things are about to get even more interesting around here.

Chapter Twenty-One

It is now Monday morning, and I couldn't be more excited. I have left thoughts of Logan and his issues behind, as well as any worries over Dante. Today is my day, and I am not going to let anyone ruin it.

I am driving along the road that leads to the marina with thoughts of all the things that I have planned for Shay whirling through my mind. I have the whole day planned, and I have left the details for the evening open to be based on the outcome of the day. If everything goes according to plan, my poor lonesome penis will be introduced to a new friend.

I pull into the spot at the marina that is designated for the boat owner. He didn't have a problem with my extending the use of his boat, as I sweetened the deal that I previously made with him. It will all be worth it. I exit my vehicle, and head around to the trunk to start unloading all the previsions that we will be needing. I have all the food in coolers, my own fishing gear, and a few surprises for Shay. It takes a few trips to the yacht and then some prep time to set the scene.

I am just finishing the last few details when I notice the time. It is now five minutes to nine, and I need to be down by the dock to wait for her. I feel like a kid at Christmas, all excitement and anticipation. I race down to the boardwalk in time to see her emerging from her car.

The site is amazing.

She slides her elegant legs out first, clad in fitted denim. Then the rest emerges. She is wearing a red, breast-hugging tank top, and a white hoodie is in her left arm. Her hair is in an adorable ponytail, with wispy, loose strands gently blowing around her face. She hasn't seen me yet, and my patience is rewarded further when she opens the back door of her car, and bends inside.

Fuck me!

Her jeans are molded to the most perfect ass in creation, and I am staring like a horny teenager at a peep show. I have to bite back a moan when she starts to wiggle as she retrieves something. I can't wait to bite into that and lick it all over. My dick notices these thoughts and is starting to become strangled in my pants. I quickly adjust myself, and then stride towards her to offer my assistance. At my approach, she straightens from the back seat and is holding some very expensive and professional looking fishing hear. Her smile rivals the sun in its brilliance. The fact that her smile is for me, makes my heart melt.

"Can I help you carry some of that?" I ask.

She is still smiling, but is beginning to look a little dazed. I almost forgot my own attire for the day, which I specifically chose with her in mind.

I have on a pair of light-wash blue jeans, faded in all the right places, and a black muscle-shirt, which is molded to my chest like a lover. I take care of my body, and have a physique that shows it. I was hoping that she would appreciate my efforts, and by the hungry looks she is now giving me, I succeeded.

Score!

"Oh, um, yes that would be great." She is still just standing there with her fishing rod and tackle box, so I take pity on her and gently remove the box from her delicate fingers.

This seems to snap her out of her trance, and she blushes a beautiful shade of pink. I can think of another part of her body that would look good wearing that shade, perhaps after a naughty spanking?

Wrong thought to have, as I am now hard enough to impale plaster!

I smile at her, and ask if there is anything else that she needs to bring. She shakes her head in the negative, but her gaze has now dropped to my crotch, and I watch her pupils dilate.

Yes, there isn't much left to the imagination, as I am on display through these jeans. She licks her lips, and I almost toss her tackle box aside and pounce on her. It takes a herculean effort, but I manage to ask her to follow me. My voice may have been a bit strangled, along with other parts of me. If I don't get control of myself, there will be a permanent imprint of my zipper on my dick.

Oh, and just in case you're wondering, my penis is improving nicely. There is only some faded, yellow bruising left, and it isn't bent anymore.

Thank God!

We walk along together in silence, and then I stop in front of the yacht and turn to face her. "This is where we will be staying until tomorrow. I hope you like it."

She gasps, and her eyes are like saucers on her face. I can't tell if this is a good thing, or a bad thing. Her mouth is parted, and her eyes are scanning over the whole yacht. Finally, her gaze lands on mine, and I know that it is a good thing.

"This is incredible, Alex. I thought a small fishing boat for the day, and maybe your place at night, but this is amazing! I can't believe that you went to all this effort just for me."

Doesn't she know by now?

I move closer to her and place my free hand on her cheek, looking deep into her amazing blue eyes. "I would do anything to make you as happy as you make me. You are an amazing woman, and deserve to be treated like a princess. Let me be your Prince Charming, and I will make all of your fairytales come true."

Her eyes become a bit misty, but she blesses me with one of the most beautiful smiles yet.

"How has some lucky woman not made you hers?"

"I believe my heart was waiting for yours."

A single tear escapes her eye, and I gently wipe it from her soft cheek. This woman is turning me into a walking advertisement for Hallmark, and I wouldn't change a thing.

Still stroking her cheek, I bend down and feather my lips over hers. This moment is about tenderness, and I let my lips convey the vulnerable emotions that my voice cannot say.

She eagerly engages in the exchange of tender brushes of lips and tongue. I allow myself to linger for few moments more, and then reluctantly back away. I smile down at her, and ease my hand down to twine with hers. I turn towards the yacht, and with a gentle tug on her hand, we board the boat.

☺

We spend the morning taking the boat on a lazy journey around the bay. It's still a bit too brisk to set anchor and begin our day of fishing, so we enjoy the ride and chat together while taking in the scenery.

She tells me that her mother absolutely loves the flowers that I sent, and her dad wasn't given a choice about agreeing that my gesture was kind and in good taste. I still don't think that he will be singing my praises anytime soon, but at least I might have moved out of the dog house. She also tells me all about her article, and that she is almost finished. She says that she has gotten amazing praise from her editor on what she has so far, and thinks that she should be able to submit it by the end of the week.

I will be sad to not be able to see her at work anymore, but I am more relieved than anything that I won't have to worry about all the schmucks there hitting on her. She also says that she will be sad to leave, but the agreement was for the article. I tell her that we will still have plenty of time to see each other, and she agrees. Both our jobs are fairly flexible, and our schedules are pretty open.

I gird my loins to ask her about the discussion that she's going to have with her parents, regarding her getting her own place. She deflates some when she tells me that she can't do it, and also she thinks that maybe her dad would think that I have something to do with her decision.

Good God. That thought never crossed my mind!

I am rather attached to my balls, and wouldn't like seeing them displayed in her father's office with all his trophies.

It would make our dating easier if she had her own place, but I think she made the right decision. Also, if things become serious between us, I would probably just mover her in with me.

Whoa!

Did I just think that?

Having a woman go, where no woman has gone before?

I digest this for a few moments, waiting for the panic to hit me. When it doesn't, I actually find myself liking that idea.

Something to think about later.

We find a nice secluded spot, and set down the anchor. We decide to have our lunch on the deck. Our chef from the restaurant has really outdone himself and made enough scrumptious food to last us several days. I choose an assortment of meats, cheeses, fruits and homemade breads. I also grab the champagne that I had chilling and set us up a nice cozy picnic. The front deck is spacious, and has a sheltered section with some comfortable lounges, chairs, and tables. I set the scene, and then bring her up from the command room. She gushes over the lavish spread that I have displayed for us. I take her hand and lead her to where I want her to sit, right beside where I will be. I pour us each a flute of champagne, and then raise my glass to her in a toast.

"To the beautiful woman beside me, who has made me hers."

Her eyes flare at the mention of her own words, back at her. I watch her slender throat as she swallows, and then drop my eyes further to her chest as she takes a deep breath. Her breasts are round and plump, and I can't wait to have them spilling into my hands.

"To the amazing man beside me, who has taken the man of my dreams and made him a reality."

At her words, my eyes fly back up to her face. I feel a lump in my throat. I hope that I can be the man of her dreams, for she has surpassed any ideals I may have had for the woman of my own.

Our eyes are locked together, with spoken and unspoken words between us. The moment is magical, and I want to freeze it and remember every detail. The way the sun is kissing her skin, the wind caressing her hair, and the way that her eyes are sparkling bluer than the water surrounding us. I don't want to speak another word and shatter the bubble that we are in, so I just tap my glass to hers, and we both take a sip without ever breaking eye-contact.

This moment will be the one that I remember realizing that I was no longer falling, I had already fallen in love with her.

☺

It turns out, that Shay is a pro at fishing. I am no slouch, but she put my skill and knowledge to shame. She credited her abilities to her dad, which I already knew, but I listened intently like I didn't. She obviously loves her dad, a lot, and has a deep and meaningful bond with him. Great for her, but that will make my position look even more like a threat to her father. I am beginning to see why he is opposed to the idea of her dating, because he is afraid of losing her to another man. Realizing this doesn't make me feel any better, but it helps me to see where he is coming from. I need to convince him that I would never take his place in her heart, I just want my own little piece of it.

We keep one of the fish that Shay catches. Mine are too small to be even considered a snack, let alone a meal.

I am no gourmet chef, but I am not without skills. I plan on pan-frying the fish in herb and garlic, and then serving it with steamed asparagus and new baby potatoes. There is a Tiramisu already made, by our chef, in the freezer. I have a tossed salad already prepared with a red wine dressing.

Impressed, aren't you?

I pack away our fishing gear, and encourage Shay to get comfortable while I take the fish inside to prepare for our dinner. I was coming back up the stairs from the galley kitchen, when what my vision beholds causes me to stumble on my assent.

Shay has taken off her jeans and her top, and she is laying on one of the sun lounges in nothing but a black, string bikini. The triangles of the top are barely containing her mounds of glorious flesh. I can clearly see that the breeze has stiffened her nipples, and I begin to feel a part of me stiffen as well. Her stomach is toned, yet has a soft curve, and her hips flare out to hold the tiny strings of the bottom half of her bikini. I am pretty sure that my tongue is hanging out, as all that it wants to do is lick, and my eyes are devouring the feast of flesh before me.

The woman is magnificent!

I manage to recover myself and approach her at the lounge. She puts her hand up to shield her eyes when she looks up at me.

"Hey, I hope you don't mind. The sun was getting hot and I wanted to get some color, and then maybe go for a swim?"

Mind?

I am wanting to fall at her feet and thank her!

"I don't mind at all, and a swim sounds great."

I may have sounded a bit squeaky there.

She just smiles, and then rolls over.

If the sight from the front was magnificent, the sight from the back is spectacular!

Her bathing suit is failing to completely cover the generous cheeks of her ass. It is perfectly heart-shaped, and I can feel drool gathering in my mouth. The cleft between her cheeks is visible through the material, and I want to run my finger down it. I hear a stifled giggle, and realize that she knows the effect that she is having on me, and enjoying herself.

Well, two can play at that game!

I casually stroll over to the lounge beside her, and wait until she turns her head and peeks at me from between her lashes. Then, I begin my own show.

I grasp the hem of my muscle shirt and slowly drag it up and over my chest. I hear a soft gasp, but cannot see her reaction as the shirt is now being drawn over my head. When the shirt has cleared my line of vision, I can see that she isn't even trying to hide her ogling. She has turned her body completely towards me now, and is running her appreciative eyes all over my chest.

I might have flexed a little.

After I have discarded the shirt, I rest my hands on either side of my jean's zipper, and slowly move my hands up, and pop open the button. She has taken her bottom lip between her teeth, and is breathing heavily. Enjoying the power I have over her, I lower the zipper of my jeans, a few teeth at a time. By the time I reach the bottom, she is whimpering.

I smile to myself. This is fun.

With a flourish, I drop my pants and kick them aside. She is sitting up now, and has her hands balled into fists at her side while she looks her fill. I have on a pair of dark-green swim trunks, and I am pretty sure that my penis just waved at her. She slowly stands and looks up into my eyes. Her pupils are fully blown now, and my breathing is getting as erratic as hers.

"Alex, the sun is really strong. I think you need some sunscreen on, you know, so you don't burn."

She is blushing by the end of this.

Adorable.

Never let it be said that I don't give a woman what she wants. I wink at her, showing a cockiness that I am not really feeling, and then lay down on the lounge, giving her my back. I wait a few moments, and just when I fear that maybe she was joking, I hear the sound of a bottle being squeezed. Seconds later, her soft and gentle hands are being placed on my back. I close my eyes, and enjoy the feel of her touching my skin. I have given plenty of sensual massages over the years, but have never actually received one.

I didn't know what I was missing!

It feels glorious, as her hands smooth all the lotion over my skin. She pays extra attention to my arms and shoulders.

Yes, they are developed nicely.

When she makes her way down my back, I almost ask her to rub my bum. The idea of having her hands on my ass is such a hot one, I can feel a solid lump forming beneath me. Maybe not then, as I would be laying on my dick and might hurt it. I really hope that everything has healed on the inside, because there is no way that I am going to last until Thursday.

I had every intention of making tonight about Shay and pampering and pleasuring her, but I am pretty sure that my penis has other plans.

Chapter Twenty-Two

The afternoon is glorious. We indeed go swimming, and that is an exercise in control as well.

We splash and play in the water, and I am having more fun than I can remember ever having with a woman. After spending some time swimming, we decide to head back to shower and start dinner.

I almost fall off the ladder when I climb it behind her.

Those incredible legs, her delectable derriere, and the graceful movement of her body almost give me a heart attack as I try to follow her up. I lose my grip on the ladder a few times. When I finally make it up and back on the boat, my heart stutters at the sight of her. Her skin is covered in rivulets of water, gently rolling down her body. The bathing suit is now plastered to her like a second skin, leaving very little to the imagination. I feel my heart thud back into gear, and send all the blood in my body to inflate my dick. I have never seen a more glorious sight, and when I finally get her naked, I'm not sure my heart will be able to take it.

I'm going to end up dead at this rate!

My penis is harder than I can ever remember him being, and I really needed to get a grip, literally.

Taking the edge off in the shower is going to be the only way to survive the rest of the day, so I turn and tell her over my shoulder that I'm going to hit the shower first, so I can start dinner while she's having her shower. She smiles and nods back at me, and I speed off to take matters into my own hands.

☺

We are relaxing on the bow of the ship, and sipping the wine that we had with dinner. Shay seems impressed with my culinary skills, which I was hoping for. Women want a man that can cook, that way it doesn't fall solely on their shoulders. The conversation through dinner was light, but we seem to have developed our relationship to a point where we can just enjoy each other's company without filling it with idle chatter.

If someone had told me a month ago that I would be this content being in a woman's company, while clothed, I would have laughed my ass off.

Shay has changed me in the short amount of time that we have been dating, and I can honestly say that I don't want to go back to the way I was before her. If she decides to end things between us, it is going to hurt. I have never been vulnerable with a woman like this, and it is a scary feeling. If this is what Logan was referring to, I am beginning to understand why he doesn't want to do it again.

I think that I owe him an apology.

"The stars are so beautiful out here."

I start at the sound of her voice, I'm so wrapped in my own head. I glance over at her, and suck in my breath.

She is the beautiful sight out here. After her shower, she changed into a blue sundress, with a white lace jacket over it. Her hair is piled atop her head, exposing the line of her elegant neck. The light from the candles surrounding us is reflected in her eyes, and also casts her face in a soft glow. I could happily spend the rest of my life staring at her. She is the most beautiful woman I have ever been with. I feel like the luckiest bastard in the world tonight. I pick up the hand she was resting on her leg, and bring it to my mouth for a kiss. I close my eyes and savor the feel of her silky skin against my lips, and the sweet smell of her so close to me. I open my eyes and look deeply into hers.

"The stars don't even rival the beauty I am looking at."

Listen to the romance I'm spouting!

I didn't know that I had it in me, but Shay seems to bring out a side of me that I didn't know I had.

It is her turn to suck in her breath. She smiles gently, and leans closer to me before she speaks. "Alex, you had better be careful with that silver tongue of yours."

"Hmmm….or you will find a better use for it?"

She snorts, but becomes serious once more. "There is that, but I meant that you had better be careful, or I might end up falling for you."

"I hope so, because I have already fallen for you."

She inhales sharply, and then blinks her eyes rapidly.

She searches my face for the honesty of my statement, so I let her see everything I feel for her. I know when she sees it, because her face lights up with an inner glow that has nothing to do with the candle light.

"Alex, I want you, no, I need you. Make love to me, please?"

Yes!

I feel like shouting to the world that I am going to have sex, but that might ruin the moment. So, I just smile and tug her up by the hand, so she is now pressed against me, and can feel how eager I am to fulfill her request.

"As you wish."

She smiles, getting the reference to *The Princess Bride*. Then I am scooping her into my arms and carrying her off, hopefully, for the performance of my life!

☺

I have to admit, I am suffering from a wee bit of nerves by the time I get us to the bed chamber.

I slowly lower her to the floor, enjoying the slide of her body against mine. I left a bed lamp on, you know, just in case. She is looking at me now, and no woman has ever looked at me this way before. Like I am everything, and I can feel sweat breaking out on my back. I want this to be perfect for her, but I am nervous about her expectations, and my performance. I have never had this problem before, but I want this to be special.

I'm also a little unsure about how The Big Guy is going to handle his first ride after The Incident. I know that he has been fine for the two solo missions, but this is different. Also, he still isn't looking like his usual, attractive self, and I don't know how she is going to react to this.

I need to do something besides just stand here, so I take her face in my hands and lean down to kiss her. She sighs against my lips, and I need no further encouragement.

The kiss starts off with gentle explorations of our lips, and then our tongues seem to meet at the same time. It is like a fuse has been lit, and from one heartbeat to the next, the kiss becomes carnal.

I am grinding my lips against hers, and mimicking with my tongue what I want to do with another part of my body. She is mewling, and making eager noises in the back of her throat now. My blood is on fire, and my hands begin to wander her wonderful curves. I am kneading the globes of her ass, and pulling her closer to my throbbing erection. I grind myself against her, and the friction just about rolls my eyes back in my head.

Thank God I rubbed one off in the shower earlier or I would probably embarrass myself right now.

She has let her own hands come into play, and is gripping my biceps. The pain of her sharp little nails only inflames my desire for her. I move one hand away from her shapely ass, allow it to travel up her back, and around to the underswell of her breast. I slowly cup the fullness of her, and I feel her pebbled nipple against my palm.

Now I am the one making eager noises.

This seems to be a trigger for her, and she reaches between us for the buttons on my dress shirt. I also changed and dressed in dinner clothes after my shower. I am wearing a white, button-down shirt, with a pair of black dress pants.

She makes fast work of the buttons, and then her eager hands are on my chest. Letting the hand that was in "boob heaven" travel to her shoulder, I gently ease the strap on her left shoulder down. Her skin here is as soft as silk, and I let my fingers linger a moment. I finesse my mouth away from hers, and begin planting kisses down the column of her neck. She is panting and running her hands everywhere she can reach on my skin. There is a trail of heat left behind from her hands as she maps my body.

My eyes are closed at the exquisite sensations that she is creating. I gradually make my way to her shoulder, and gently bite the spot where it meets the cords of her neck, knowing that this is a sensitive spot. She gasps, and tilts her head further, for better access.

I smile against her skin, and then do it again.

She is undulating against me, and I can't wait for her to do this without the barrier of our clothes in the way. I bring my other hand up from where it has still been fondling her ass, and slowly lower her other strap. I move my head to the other side of her neck, and begin the same treatment there.

It takes me a moment to realize that she has moved her hands to the front of our bodies again, and is starting to unbuckle my belt. Wanting to distract her and slow this down, I lower the front of her dress, but suck in air when I see what I have revealed.

She is wearing a white, strapless bra that is transparent. Her breasts are lifted towards me, like an offering. I let out a strangled moan and dip my head to capture her ripe flesh with my mouth, through the material. I close my lips around her straining nipple, and roll it between my teeth. She moans, and arches against me, forgetting her task with my belt like I hoped. I begin rhythmically sucking her pebbled bud in my mouth, and her moans turn louder. Music to my ears. I switch to the other breast and give it the same treatment. I slowly lean back to study my handiwork. The material around her nipples is wet from my mouth, and her nipples are red, and jutting against the material.

Nice!

I look into her eyes, making sure that she is okay with this so far. Her pupils have almost swallowed her beautiful, blue irises. Definitely okay, then.

I reach around to her back, and unclasp her bra, without breaking eye-contact. I feel her bra release, but don't take my eyes from her face. She lowers her arms and lets the bra slide off her body, to the floor. I finally let my eyes travel to where they are aching to go. Her breasts are the stuff that fantasies are made of. Full, round globes, perfectly shaped for a man's hands, my hands. I take both breasts in my hands, and gently mold them. She makes a purring sound, and I swear I feel it in my dick. My mouth is watering for the taste of those nipples, so I bend and suck one into my mouth. Her taste was hampered by the material of the bra, as was the texture. Her taste explodes across my tongue, and this time I moan. I begin to suck, hard. She doesn't seem to mind the aggressive suction, and becomes frantic.

She is moaning and writhing for me, and I love it!

After both nipples have had my attention, I slide her dress the rest of the way down her body, as it has been pooled around her waist until now. She gracefully steps out of it, and stands proudly before me in nothing but a white thong. I am humbled by this goddess before me. The fact that she is allowing me the pleasure of her body, leaves me breathless with anticipation and awe.

I am silently thanking God for this gift.

She slowly moves into my body and reaches for my belt again. This time, I allow her to undo it. She then pops the button on my pants, and lowers the zipper. The release of pressure against my penis is much appreciated, and it springs forward, as much as my boxers will allow. She slowly runs the tips of her nails down my shaft, and I groan. I quickly shed my shirt, and then finish what she started by removing my pants and kicking them away. I stand and let her look her fill.

Her eyes are wide, and her lips are parted. In a trance-like state, she moves back in, and places her lips on my chest. The feel of her lips upon my skin makes my knees tremble. She gives me gentle kisses across my pecs, and finds one of my nipples, which she then delivers the most erotic of nibbles to.

I am about two seconds away from tossing her to the bed, ripping away the final barriers between us, and sinking into the paradise I know I will find between her supple thighs. She leans away from my chest, and looks up into my eyes while taking my hand.

She is smiling a seductive, kitten smile and leading me to the bed. I follow eagerly, more than ready to take this to the next level. She stops at the side of the bed, and God help me, she crawls across it and lays down in the middle, holding out her hand to me.

I am trembling before her, but take her hand and follow her down.

My angel.

Mine.

Chapter Twenty-Three

I ease my weight into the bed, and lie down beside her. I prop my head in my hand, and take in the sight of all this beauty, laid out beside me. I don't usually let the woman take the lead. As I mentioned earlier, I am an alpha in the bedroom. For some reason though, I am waiting for her to dictate the pace. I am so focused on her happiness and pleasure that I want her to be as comfortable and confident as she can be.

She smiles warmly and reaches over to trace the line of my jaw. I lean in to her touch and she strokes my cheek. I have never had tender moments during sex before, and I am finding that I really like it.

I reach over and lightly trace my fingers along the line of her delicate collarbone. She shivers at my touch, and I can feel my pulse quicken at her reaction. I haven't been this absorbed in eliciting a genuine reaction from a woman because of something that I was doing until now. Sure, I wanted them to enjoy themselves, but it never meant as much to me as it does with Shay.

I want to say so many things to her, but don't want to break the magic of the moment.

She lowers her hand to my chest, and gently pushes me to my back.

Hell yeah!

She leans over my upper body, with her own, and gently kisses me. If I wasn't laying down, I might have been weak in the knees, I was that affected by her. I kiss her back, just as tenderly. She slides her lips down to my chin and neck, leaving a blazing trail where her lips have been. She kisses my muscled pecs, and then lower. My six-pack is getting special attention, and I can feel my dick is straining to reach for her through the boxers.

She notices, and giggles softly.

I don't have time to become embarrassed, because she leans back, gives me a wink, then lifts and pulls my boxers away from me. She pulls them down to the tops of my thighs, and then studies what she has uncovered.

I am looking at what she is, but we are having different reactions.

I wince, looking at a penis that is intimidating in its coloring and bulging veins. The bruising isn't really noticeable, with the flush that is covering it from all the blood pounding down there. I am a fairly well-endowed guy, but this is more than I have ever seen of myself, and I can only imagine what a delicate thing like Shay is thinking.

I chance a look at her face, and stop short.

It is not terror or repulsion that she is exhibiting, but breathless awe.

I blink my eyes, because that can't be right, but nothing on her face changes.

She is looking at my dick like it is the biggest piece of chocolate, and she can't wait to gobble it up.

Well, if I was another guy, I might have preened a bit.

Fine, I preened a bit.

She licks her lips, and then looks up at me with wide eyes. Her breaths are puffing out of her lips, in a shallow rhythm. My dick, not wanting to be forgotten, gives a jerk to draw her attention back to him. She looks back down, and an impish smile spreads across her sexy, plump lips. I am visualizing what those juicy lips would feel like around my throbbing length, when she leans down and makes my fantasy a reality.

My hips shoot up, without any of my control, at the first contact of her moist lips parting around my sensitive tip. My eyes are in the back of my head, so I can't enjoy the sight, but I can feel, oh can I feel! I don't remember a time I was so sensitive. Must have something to do with having an erection since this morning. Even being in the cold water for our swim, only took me from a full, throbbing hard-on, to a semi.

My thoughts fizzle out, as she begins to work my aching flesh. Tingles are running up and down my spine, and wrapping around my balls. Her tongue is fluttering on the underside, as she bobs, and I can't help the involuntary thrusting my hips are doing. I don't want to gag her, and am trying to keep my thrusts shallow, but I am fighting for control of my body. I make the mistake of forcing my eyes downward, and the sight of her lips parted around my cock, glistening with her saliva, almost brings my release.

I have to do something or this show will be over before it has really begun.

I gently grab her head with one hand and myself with the other. I slowly pull her off me, and my dick pops free of her mouth.

She looks up at me, and pouts.

She pouts at me!

Could she be any more adorable?

I smile down at her and signal for her to lay down.

My turn!

I sit up and lean over her body to pay homage to her beautiful breasts again. I hold one of her breasts to my mouth and suck a nipple inside it. She arches her back and starts to make those purring noises again. I smile against her nipple and give it a love bite. She gasps, but soon moans afterwards. My girl has a little kinky streak. Good to know. I give the other breast some love, and then start my own journey to the *Promised Land*. I kiss down to her navel and spend a few moments licking in and out of her belly button. She shivers for me again and I love how responsive her body is. I slide around so that I am now able to remove my boxers, and I kneel between her soft, womanly thighs.

My erection is bobbing between us, but I am more focused on her right now.

I bend down and lick around the top of her thong. It is her hips lifting off the mattress now. I use my teeth to gently pull her panties down, exposing her as I go.

Jesus!

She is completely waxed, and all her female parts are perfectly visible.

I almost swallow my tongue!

I release her thong from my teeth and drag them the rest of the way down her legs with my hands. I have to move to one side to get them off, but then I am back where I am dying to be. I lay down on my stomach, anticipation thick in my mouth. I put my hands on the inside of her thighs and gently urge her to open the doors to heaven.

She is pretty and pink here, and she is glistening for me.

I know I am staring, but I can't help it.

I am a guy, and we are visual creatures.

The sight before me has rendered me immobile. I take a deep breath, and then I bend to her swollen folds. I give an experimental lick, and she bows off the bed.

Yes!

I do it again and start to explore her with my mouth and tongue, finding what drives her the wildest. I find a spot that makes her hips roll and her legs shake. While keeping my focus on that area, I insert a finger to her snug depths and stroke her, finding her g-spot. In a flash, her hips shoot up off the bed, bowing her back, and her legs clamp around my head. She is screaming her pleasure, shaking from the force of her orgasm.

I feel like a god!

I gentle, and slow what I am doing, bringing her down. I milk her orgasm for all it is worth, and when she is laying pliant and sated, I crawl up her body. I want to look into her eyes and remind her who just made her feel this way.

It is a guy thing.

Our egos need stroking just as much as our dicks.

I brace myself above her and look into her passion-glazed eyes. I feel like thumping my chest and sending out smoke signals to everyone I know. She is focusing on me, smiling, and I feel my heart squeeze in my chest.

I know it seems fast, but I am so in-love with this woman. It has to be love because I have never felt anything even close to this before. I brush her hair from her face, lean in and kiss her bee-stung lips. She must have been biting them for they are even plumper than before. I nibble the bottom one with my teeth and then lick away the sting with my tongue. She moans and wraps her arms around me. As the kiss deepens, I realize that my penis is working independent of my brain and trying to align himself for entry. With a growl, I break the kiss and reach over to the bedside table, wrenching the drawer open so that I can grab a condom from the string I put there earlier. Shay shifts, and puts her hand on my arm to stop me.

Puzzled, and a little panicked, I look back to her.

"It is okay, Alex. I am on the pill and I don't want anything between us. If that is alright with you?"

Bareback?

I feel a shudder work its way through my body. I have never taken a woman that way. But then, she isn't just any woman, is she?

"You're sure?"

"More than sure. Please, Alex. I want you, all of you."

I close my eyes, because there must have been some dust in them.

Okay, so, maybe she just made me tear-up a bit. I will not admit this to anyone, though!

"Then you have me, all of me, including my heart."

I open my eyes to see that she now has tears in her eyes as well. She is smiling at me like I just hung the moon for her. I could get used to her looking at me like this.

"Don't you know? You already have mine."

Before either one of us can ruin this with our tears, I lean and kiss her as I line my body up with hers and gently begin to push my way in. We both groan through the kiss, at the excruciating pleasure we are feeling. I take my time, with shallow strokes, knowing that I need to allow her to adapt to my size, especially with the extra engorging I am experiencing down there. I can feel my body shaking from the control I am maintaining to keep this slow.

After what feels like an eternity, I am fully seated in her, our groins kissing intimately. I stay there to savor the feeling of being inside of this woman. I must have been taking too long, for she lifts her hips up, indicating that I should start moving. I smile down at her and then pull almost all the way out, before sliding back in. She moans, long and loud, while I have to grit my teeth against the rising tide of pleasure. I suck in some air and then begin to move in a steady rhythm. I can feel the wet heat surrounding me, and the steady pulsing and fluttering of her channel.

It is almost more than I can take.

I lift her hips slightly for a better angle, and she starts moaning louder, encouraging me to go harder. Well, never one to disappoint a lady, I start pounding my body into hers. She screams, and launches into another orgasm. I can feel her milking my cock with the force of it, and that is all that it takes to trigger my own.

With a roar I will later be embarrassed about, I feel my orgasm blast from me in endless waves of bliss. It feels like it never ends, and I am trembling through it. I think I saw God.

I hold her to me, and pepper kisses over her face. Conscious of my weight on her, I roll to the side and take her with me, dragging her across my chest. We are both breathing hard and spent.

I just had the most amazing sexual experience of my life, with the woman I love, and my penis survived.

Yay me!

Chapter Twenty-Four

We end up making love two more times during the night, and each time seems to be better than the last. I am really happy with The Big Guy. He's a champ, and I am so relieved that there doesn't seem to be any permanent damage caused by *The Incident*. He is going to be okay.

I feel a tear trying to escape my eye.

You have no idea what a penis means to a guy, so don't judge me.

Shay is everything I could have hoped for in bed. She is fun, surprisingly kinky, seriously sexy, and has a sexual appetite that matches my own perfectly. I am so in love with her. I'm pretty sure that if we didn't already know each other, and about each other, this might not have happened so fast, but then again this is Shay. I was helpless to fall for her.

We are laying in the bed, and I know the morning must be here because the sun is peeking through the window blinds. I am holding her to me, spooned against her back. I have not had the pleasure of spooning before, as I have never spent the night with a woman.

Yes, you read that right.

I always send them away, sated and happy after the sex. I typically did not want to encourage clingers, even if I was sleeping with the same woman for a time.

I didn't know what I was missing.

The feel of all that warm, womanly flesh in my arms. Her softness snuggled up to my hardness. Like two halves of a whole, the pieces fitting together like they were made for each other.

Listen to me!

Even in my own head I sound like a sap. This woman has changed the very fabric of my being. I am not the same man that I was before her, and I am liking myself more every minute that I spend with her.

She has taken a reckless playboy and made him into a man worthy of love. At least, I hope I am worthy.

I am just enjoying the feel of her sleeping in my arms, and the smell of her hair spread out around us, when I hear my cell phone. I had put it on the nightstand to charge. Careful not to wake her, I slip my arms from around her, and gently ease from the bed. She moans a little, and then snuggles further under the blankets.

Adorable.

I snatch up my phone and leave the room, shutting the door behind me. It is cool on the boat, and I quickly look for something to put on. My carry-on bag is in the galley kitchen, so I head there to rummage for some clothes. Once I locate my bag, I grab a pair of jeans and a Henley. Once I'm dressed, I start the coffee to brew while I check my phone. There are three missed text messages and one missed phone call. The missed call is from Dante and so are two of the texts. The other text is from Logan. I decide to see what Dante has to say first. I open his first text.

Everything is done. You will not be bothered by her, or anyone else.

The relief I feel almost has me sagging to the floor. I brace myself against the counter and just take a moment before I read the next message. Shay will be safe. That is all I ever cared about.

The next text leaves me a bit chilled.

It cost me something very important. You owe me. I will let you know what I need from you, soon.

Well, fuck!

What did my friend have to do to save my ass?

I feel like an asshole that I didn't even stop to think about what he had to do, I just feel relief that he did it. I will gladly pay any price, as long as it doesn't hurt Shay. I can't see Dante wanting to hurt her either. So, whatever he wants, he will have, along with my eternal gratitude.

I open Logan's text next, and the shocks keep coming.

Laney has agreed to let me take her out, so we can discuss our situation. No promises.

Hallelujah!

If anyone can reach Logan, it is Laney. I just hope he gives her the chance. Not my problem though.

They are grown-ups, and it's time he started acting like one instead of a scared little boy. I would never say that to him, but I can think it.

I put my phone down and I am reaching into the cupboard to look for mugs, when I feel a pair of delicate arms wrap around me from behind. I jump slightly, and then sigh when I feel her press against my back and lay her head on my shoulder. I grab two mugs absently and place them on the counter. I turn in the circle of her arms so I can wrap my own around her. She is smiling up at me, and that smiling face is the most beautiful sight I have ever seen in the morning. I lean down and brush my lips against her forehead, breathing in her scent.

"Good morning, sunshine. I was just making coffee. How did you sleep?"

She smirks at me. "Well, I don't think I had much sleep, but what I did have was good."

I chuckle at her sass. I love her sass.

"I would apologize for your lack of sleep, but I'm not sorry about what kept you from sleeping."

"Wicked man. I'm not sorry either. Sleep is overrated."

I laugh out loud at that and give her a final squeeze before gesturing for her to sit at the little galley table. Once she is perched on the stool at the table, I realize what she is wearing, or more accurately, not wearing. She has taken the sheet off the bed and has it wrapped around her body.

My body stiffens, some parts more than others, at the vision she is presenting.

She looks like some sexy goddess and I want to worship her. Her hair is mussed from our sex-a-thon, her lips are puffy from my kisses, there are some whisker burns on her neck and chest, and I think I see a hickey above her left breast.

Oops!

Her body is concealed by the sheet, but her curves are very evident. What has my heart tripping in my chest though, is her eyes. They are slumberous but bright with an emotion I have only had glimpses of before. She is sitting there, baring her emotions for me through her eyes, and I suddenly have a lump in my throat. I really hope that is love that I am seeing, but I need to be sure. Time to be a man about this.

"I love you," leaps out of my mouth.

Not at all what I thought was going to come out.

Too late now, and really it is the truth anyways.

I do love her.

She gasps, and her hand flies to her mouth, her eyes wide.

I start to panic, and begin to babble. "I know it might seem too soon, but I have known you for years. Your cousin is my best-friend. I know about your life, even if I didn't get to know you until recently. You are everything that I never knew I was looking for. Your smile lights up places in me, that I didn't even know where dark. I have felt more alive in your company than I have in a long time. You are beautiful, smart, funny and incredibly sexy. You make me feel things I have never felt before, and things I only want to feel with you. How could I not love you?"

Tears are streaming down her face now and my panic worsens.

What do I do?

Yep, babble some more.

"You have made me a better man, and I like the person I am with you. I have never been in love before, and I have never told another person, besides my mom, that I love them. I want a future with you. I want a life where I am not a *me* anymore, but a *we*, and I want to be a *we* with you."

Okay, that didn't sound right, did it?

Moron!

She is sniffling delicately, and the tears are still coming.

What am I doing wrong here?

She suddenly jumps off the stool and flies into my body, wrapping her arms around me with a strength that surprises me. With nothing else to do, I wrap her up in my arms and begin stroking her back, making soothing noises. I hope they are soothing. They might sound like animal calls for all I know.

I am in uncharted territory here!

After her sniffles die down a bit, I chance a look at her face which is still pressed to my shirt. She must have felt me looking at her because she looks up at me, with her beautiful, amazing eyes that are glistening from her tears.

"Did you mean all of that?" she asks.

Umm...which parts? I'm a babbling fool and I'm not sure what's coming out of my mouth. I nod my head anyway. This seems to have been the right response. Her whole face lights up with her smile.

"Those were the most beautiful words I have ever heard. You are the most remarkable man I have met. I feel like someone plucked every desire and dream that I ever had and put you in my life to fulfil them. I have known you for half of my life, and if I am being honest, I always had a crush on you. What I felt for you as a child is nothing compared to what I feel for you now. You are more than I could have ever thought possible, and I have been falling in love with from the first time I saw you again at the club. I love you too,

Alex. I want that future with you, the one you described."

I bury my face in her neck and hug her tight.

There are two reasons for this. One, I am overwhelmed with emotion. Two, there may, or may not, have been tears in my eyes.

I am going to plead *The Fifth* on this one.

When I trust that I can speak without embarrassing myself, I whisper into her hair. "You have my heart in your hands. Everyone was so worried about me hurting you, but what they don't realize is that I would be hurting my own heart. You are everything, Shay. Everything. Move in with me?"

There I go again, letting my mouth spout off without my brain being aware of what I am saying!

What did I just do?

More importantly, how is she going to react to that verbal fart?

She pulls away from me and forces my eyes to hers by gently lifting my head, still hanging from where it had been resting against her neck.

I don't know what I am expecting to see in her eyes, but it isn't them smiling at me. "Alex, why are you acting like you just admitted to kicking a puppy? Do you regret asking?"

"God, no! I hadn't planned on just blurting that out to you, though. I have thought about it, yes, but I haven't even talked to you about your living arrangements, let alone asking that of you."

"Well, this is how I see it. I was planning on moving out of my parents' house soon anyway. If we are going to be serious about each other, it makes sense that we would have gotten to the point where we lived together eventually. That would have been the normal progression of a normal relationship, but our relationship doesn't seem to be following the usual time lines. Having said all that, I will need some more time to prepare my parents. Moving out on my own was going to be hard enough to discuss with them. Moving in with a man is going to make things a bit more challenging. Ultimately, the decision is mine, not theirs. I want their approval and support, though. Do you understand what I am trying to say?"

"I think so. You are not saying no, just not yet. I understand that you want to do this right by your parents. I respect you even more for that. I love my parents too, and my mother would never let me do anything to disappoint her. She is going to love you."

Shay giggles. "You mean your reputation with the ladies hasn't reached her ears yet? I can't see her having pride in that."

"I am still pure in my mother's eyes, so no. She is very proud of her virgin son."

Shay is laughing out right now, and I find myself laughing with her.

I try to contain my laughter so that I can get us our coffee. I pour the coffee and take the two mugs over to the table. Then I grab Shay and drag her down to my lap. She squeaks, but snuggles in against me. I am holding her with one arm and reaching for my coffee with the other, when there is a knock on the door.

Who the hell is that?

The only people who know where I am are the owner of the boat and Dante. Getting a sinking feeling in the pit of my stomach, I gently ease Shay from my lap so that I can head up the few stairs to the door that leads to the deck. I unlock and open the door.

Dante is standing on the other side. He is in his customary black clothing with motorcycle boots and his sunglasses. He gives me a nod and then removes his glasses. I don't like the look on his face.

"We need to talk."

Fuck.

Chapter Twenty-Five

I go back inside to let Shay know that Dante needs to talk to me. She just smiles and says that she will finish her coffee and then grab a shower.

Damn, I'm going to miss having sexy shower time with her.

Dante better have a good reason for being here.

Stomping back up the stairs, I may have opened the door a bit too aggressively. It thumps angrily against the wall.

My bad.

Dante is sitting at the table outside, the one that Shay and I were sitting at the night before. He is giving off the impression of being relaxed, but I can see the lines of tension around his mouth and eyes.

Sighing, I let my anger drain. This is my friend, who just did me a huge favor, at a personal cost to himself. I have no right to feel anything negative towards him. I approach him, and take the seat across from him. I look at him expectantly. He seems to gather himself, and if anything, looks even tenser. This is not going to be good.

"I am about to tell you some things, things that you cannot repeat to anyone, especially Logan."

Nope, not good.

"Okay, but I don't want to know, and then have to keep something from him that might hurt him."

"Well, I am not sure about it hurting him, but he will not be happy about it." It sounded like he said, "more like pissed" under his breath.

"Alright, but first I want to thank you for what you did for me, and by association, Shay. Whatever you need, all you have to do is ask."

"You are welcome, and we will get to that. I have to tell you a few things first, though." Here he takes a deep breath, and pins me with a direct gaze. "It has to do with the case I was working on, the one that I couldn't tell you about. It was Lissa."

Now, I suck in a breath. Logan's sister. He is super protective of her, and I can't imagine how Dante thinks we can keep anything about her from Logan, much less how he will react if he finds out we kept something about her from him.

"It also has to do with me."

Oh shit!

I am getting a very bad feeling here, and if he is saying what I think he is, Logan is going to have a fit.

There has to be another explanation.

"Just tell me." I can't stand the suspense.

"She had a stalker. She came to my buddy, the one who runs the private security company, and also private investigations. He asked me to follow the guy. I didn't realize that it was Lissa who was the client, yet. I found pictures of her all over his apartment ... some were very intimate."

Oh my God!

I can literally feel all the blood draining from my face. Lissa is like a little sister to all of us. I am starting to feel sick. I hope this ends with Dante beating the shit out of the guy because if Logan finds out, well, he might not stop at the beating.

"I wanted Lissa to be safe, so I had no choice but to approach her, and let her know that I was the one handling her case. She freaked, naturally. She didn't want any of us knowing, which is why she went to my friend, who is big on discretion. Anyway, we talked, and came to an agreement on where she would hide until this guy was taken care of."

Oh no!

"She has been staying at my place."

Fuck!

"I know what you are thinking, but please wait until this story is over before you fillet my balls."

I nod, but I what I want to do is ask him if he has lost his damned mind?

Logan is going to kill him!

"I told you that I had information that the gang who was after you would want. It also happens that Lissa's stalker owed them money, and they have been looking for him. I wanted to handle her stalker personally, but I turned his location over to Kylie's cousin in exchange for him to leave you alone. I also had a little chat with him about his psycho cousin. Seems this isn't the first time that she has lied to him about a guy. I would not want to be her right now. Gangs might be unlawful, but they have a strict code with each other and do not suffer liars lightly."

"Wait a minute, if they now know that she is lying, why would you have to give them anything?"

"They wouldn't have dropped it just because I asked them, they don't work that way. Yes they know she is lying now, but in order to meet with them, I had to have something they wanted. It is just the way things work on the streets."

"I understand your need to protect Lissa, we are all protective of her, but what difference does it make who takes the guy out? Good riddance, and this way your hands stay clean."

Dante growls at me.

He actually growled.

He suddenly looks capable of murder, and I might have peed a little. I back away from him slightly, and I am sure my eyes are showing white from being so wide.

"He was mine to punish. Mine!"

"Okay, I get it. Calm the fuck down, man."

After he takes several deep breaths, he appears to reign in the murderous rage he was feeling.

"No, I don't think you do get it. How would you feel if someone was peeping, and perving on your woman, and terrifying her while doing it?"

"I would probably be locked up for murder, but that is because she is my woman. I would hurt someone on Lissa's behalf, but Logan is the one who would be capable of murder if someone was threatening his sister. Why are we not telling him again?"

"Mostly, because she begged me not to."

"Mostly?"

"The main reason is because I don't feel very brotherly towards Lissa, and I think she feels the same way."

"Oh shit!"

"Exactly."

"We can't let him find out."

"Agreed."

"At least until your children graduate."

"Don't be an asshole. I am not going to risk my friendship with him until I figure out what may, or may not, happen with Lissa. Also, he can't find out about her stalker, because then he will find out where she has been staying. What a cluster fuck."

"That about sums it up. But don't you think he will be even more pissed when he finds out that we didn't tell him?"

"That is for Lissa to tell him, if she ever feels he needs to know. Right now, he doesn't need to know."

"Okay, what is the favor then?"

His cheeks become tinged with pink.

Oh my God, he is blushing!

I have never seen Dante blush before. He is too volatile right now to poke with that stick, so I will tuck it away for a future date.

"Lissa is really close with, Shay. They are more like sisters, than cousins."

I nod my head. I already know this. I indicate with my hand that he should continue. If possible, he turns a deeper shade of pink.

Priceless!

"Well, I was hoping that she could talk to Lissa."

I have a feeling I know where this is going, but I am having too much fun watching him squirm. "About what, in particular?"

"Me."

Oh man!

I wish I could torment him a bit more, but I can see how much this is embarrassing him.

"About how she may, or may not, feel towards you?"

He gives a jerky nod of his head, and then begins to look anywhere but at me.

Yeah, I can just imagine how uncomfortable this is making him. Guys don't talk about feelings. It's on the Man Card.

"Is this the favor?'

Another nod.

"Then, no."

His eyes whip back to mine, and the look on his face is worth it!

I almost snicker. Almost.

"No?"

"I am not doing it as a favor for what you did. I will do it as your friend. You can keep your favor for another time."

It takes him a moment to realize what I just said, probably because he is still stuck on, "no". When he realizes what I am saying, he smiles.

Damn, if I was batting for the other team, well, you know. He has a great smile.

I will leave it at that.

"Thanks, man. That means a lot. I feel like I am back in high school, asking one of my friends if the popular girl likes me."

I chuckle at that. We are definitely in mangina territory here.

"No problem, although I am pretty sure that you never had a problem with the girls in high school. All you would have had to do is bat those chocolate eyes of yours, with the disgustingly long lashes, and even the female teachers would have thrown their panties at you."

He is laughing now, which is what I was going for. "Are you hitting on me?"

"Only if you will respect me in the morning." I blow him a kiss.

He is belly laughing now. "You are an idiot, but thanks, I think."

"Thank me after I have sent Shay on her secret mission. By the way, how much do I tell her?"

"Nothing about the stalker. That is for Lissa to tell her, if she wants. Just ask her if she can find out if there is even a chance that I should pursue anything with Lissa."

"Done, but I have to ask. How did this happen?"

"That, my friend, is something I am still working out."

"Fair enough. I can relate, because I didn't see it coming with Shay either. I'm still sorting through all that I feel for her and how it happened."

"I am not touching that one."

"I love her."

You would have thought that I said I just dumped a body overboard by the way he reacted.

Is it that hard to believe I am capable of loving someone?

Before I can get too upset, he lets out a *whoop*.

Okay, then. That's better.

"That is great! Does she feel the same way?"

"Yes, and I asked her to move in with me, which compared to you, must seem slow, since you already have a woman living with you." I smirk.

That was a good one.

"My situation is not the same as yours, and you know it. Dick." He is smiling, though. "Not one to waste time, are you? What did she say?"

"I know it seems fast, but it just feels right. I can't explain it any better than that. She says that she wants to ease her parents into it though, and I respect that."

Dante makes a strangled sound before he speaks. "Oh man, it was nice knowing you. Her dad is going to have your balls. I would love to be a fly on the wall for that conversation."

"Thanks for the vote of confidence, but I happen to agree with you. I hope Shay can work some magic with him, or you will be planning my funeral."

"Nah, it won't come to that. I can't see him being too thrilled about it, but what can he do? She is an adult, and he can't really stop her. He might huff, and puff, but in the end, he will have no choice but to deal with it. She is his daughter, and all he really wants is her happiness. If you make her happy, he will see that, and come around."

"I hope so. Maybe I should ask him to that soccer game before she talks to them. I can let him know how much she means to me, in a public place, where he can't maim me."

Dante snorts. "Have fun with that."

"Hey, you should be more sympathetic to my cause. You are going to have to deal with Logan if you start dating his sister. I am guessing that he will make his uncle look like a teddy bear in comparison."

The smile is gone from his face now, and he is looking paler by the second, which is saying something considering he has an olive complexion.

He looks down at his lap and then looks back up at me. "I don't want to lose a friend, but I am not going to let him ruin the chance that I might have with Lissa."

"Then we don't let either of those possibilities happen."

I wish I felt as confident as I sounded. Judging by the look on Dante's face, he isn't feeling it either.

Shit, meet fan.

Chapter Twenty-Six

Being back in the real world again sucks.

I enjoyed that little cocoon that Shay and I had been in on the boat. After Dante leaves, I go back in to find her all showered and packed. She says that she needs to get home and get some work done. I understand, but I'm still disappointed. Once I have taken my own shower, get dressed and packed, I whip together a light breakfast for us. She says that she could have done it, but the idea of her cooking for me...well, it would have led to other things and we're on a schedule.

We have a passionate goodbye at our cars, and I may have tried to convince her to play hooky. She lets me down gently and promised that we can have dinner together the following night. In the end, I agree. We get into our separate vehicles and go on our separate ways.

Then, I am miserable.

After spending all that time with her, I'm rather lonely.

Another first for me.

It is now Tuesday night and I am vegging in my living room, trying to concentrate on the crime show that I put on. It is just making me think of Dante.

What a pickle he has gotten himself into.

I know that we don't have control over our feelings for others, but I am sure he could have found someone other than Logan's sister to start having feelings for.

Listen to me. Like I am one to talk. I fell for his cousin.

Poor Logan. First his cousin, now his sister. He is going to wonder why we had to keep it in his family. It's not like there aren't other women out there, it just happens that we have our sights on the two women that are in his life and mean the most to him. It's a good thing that he doesn't have a mother anymore, or she might have been in the mix too.

Okay, probably not, but you get my meaning.

I am just about to turn the TV off and head to my office, when I hear a knock at the door.

Who could that be at this time of night?

I get up from the couch and walk over to the door to look through the peephole.

Staring back at me is Logan.

Shit, fuck, and hell!

What does he want, and how am I going to look him in the eyes knowing what I do?

I take in a deep breath for courage, and open the door.

He doesn't bother saying anything, just squeezes past me and heads into the kitchen. I shut the door and follow him. He is opening cupboards and rummages around. After a few minutes of this, he turns to me with a scowl.

"Where do you keep your scotch? I know that you have some, so don't bother lying. You always have a bottle of that fancy, Scottish stuff around."

"That fancy, Scottish stuff is called Balvenie. It is whiskey, not scotch, and I don't keep it in my kitchen."

"Whatever, where is it?"

"Why? You don't like it."

"I don't care, I just need a drink."

"I am not going to get you a drink until you tell me why you need a drink at..." I look at my watch. "...10:30 on a Tuesday night?"

He storms past me, shooting me a dirty look over his shoulder.

Lovely.

I follow him into the living room just as he throws himself into one of the chairs. He is sprawled over it, one of his arms thrown over his face.

Seriously?

Drama queen.

I shake my head at the display and head to my liquor cabinet to get him his damn drink. It is obvious that I will not be getting anything out of him without it.

After pouring a small amount of whiskey into a glass, I walk over to him. His arm, the one that is not covering his eyes, shoots out towards me and signals for me to give it to him. Sighing, I place the drink in his hand. He removes the arm from his eyes, sits up, and downs the amber liquid in one gulp. His eyes begin to water, and he is coughing slightly.

"How can you drink that stuff? It tastes awful, and it burns everything in its path!"

"I happen to like the taste. And if you sip it, instead of chug it, it warms without burning."

"Well, to each their own. I personally like my esophagus and stomach lining."

I roll my eyes. "Very funny. I guess that you won't be wanting another then?"

He shudders, while saying, "Fuck no! If I wasn't so desperate, I wouldn't have had the first one."

I return to my spot on the couch and just stare at him, waiting for him to elaborate. The mulish line of his jaw lets me know that he is aware of what I am waiting for. He finally gives in though.

"I went out with Laney tonight," he finally says.

I straighten up at this and lean forward to hear more.

He starts to rub the back of his neck, indicating that whatever happened, it is stressing him.

"We met at a restaurant just around the corner from the bar. Her idea, not mine. She wanted to meet somewhere neutral. Again, her idea. I should have known not to agree to meet her so close to the bar."

Ugh, oh!

"So, we meet. It was awkward at first. I didn't know what to say to her. She tried talking to me about work, I guess to break the ice. I didn't really want to talk about work. So, like an idiot, I blurt out that I saw her with that guy the other night. She looks startled at first, and then she gets pissed. She tells me that I have no right bringing that up, and that who she dates is none of my business. I fear, that I did not handle that too well. I got mad, and told her some bullshit line about not bringing her personal life to the bar, and, well, she slapped me."

O. M. G.

Personally, I am thinking that he deserved that, but I don't say it.

"She was horrified about what she had done, and started to cry. I panicked, and then blurted out that if I wasn't so damned attracted to her, her personal life wouldn't bother me. Needless to say, that bomb stopped the tears. She was actually shocked, and that made me feel worse. I should have told her this before now. Should have found my balls and dealt with this like a man. I told her that although I was attracted to her, I was not emotionally available. She took that better than I thought she would and said that it explained a lot. So, we agreed to see how things go from now on, and that we would not see anyone else until we figured out where this thing is going. She told me that she has been attracted to me for a long time, but didn't think that I saw her as anything other than an employee. I told her that I have been attracted to her for some time as well, and tried to just see her as another employee, but that I can't do that anymore. After we discussed all this, it was easier to be there with her. We were enjoying our meal, and just talking. It was nice. Then it went to hell."

I have all sorts of scenarios playing out in my head of what might have happened, but I never would have guessed what actually did happen.

He seems to brace himself for this next part. "One of the women from the other night was at the restaurant and decided to come over to the table. Seeing me there with another woman didn't seem to bother her, and I guess it wouldn't if she could have sex with me while another woman was involved. She squeezed herself between me and the table, got comfy on my lap, and then planted a big, wet kiss on me right in front of Laney. It all happened so fast, and I was too stunned to react right away. By the time I got control of the situation, the woman was thanking me for a good time the other night with her and her *two* friends. I told you that I couldn't remember how many there were. She was apologizing for the way they all left before I woke-up. Apparently one of them left in the middle of the night because she had to work, one had left in the early morning to sneak back to her boyfriend, and the last left early in the morning to feed her cat. Laney, of course, heard the whole tale while I sat with my mouth agape. What was I supposed to say? Apparently saying nothing was the worst thing to do, because she threw some money down on the table, and stormed out before I could do anything. The woman, I don't even know her name, asked if I wanted to come home with her. I thanked her for the offer, but told her that I was off the market. She looked to the door, where Laney had stormed out, and then back at me. I could see the wheels turning, so I told her I had to go, and removed her from my lap. She just shrugged her shoulder, and then flounced away. I paid the bill for our food, got in my car, and now here I am."

Do we all have karma kicking us in the ass, or what?

How can we all have created such a mess out of our lives in such a short amount of time?

Thankfully, mine seems to be working out.

Dante still has a shit-storm ahead of him with Logan, and the fallout from that to deal with. Logan, well, I don't even know what will happen in his situation. Nothing good right now, that is for sure.

Feeling bad for my friend, I offer to talk to Laney for him. He thanks me, but says that this is his mess and he will clean it up. I offer to take him out for a few drinks, but he says that alcohol won't fix his problems and that he is just going to go home. He just needed someone to listen to him, and offer some advice. I try to make suggestions on how he should proceed, but really, I have nothing. I have never been in a situation quite like that. Given how I was with women before Shay, it is a miracle really.

I tell him to call me if he needs anything, and that I will see him tomorrow at the club to organize this week's theme. He thanks me, and promises to let me know if he thinks of anything.

After walking him out, and then shutting and locking the door, I turn everything off, and head to bed. I figure I might need a good night's rest, because God only knows what will happen tomorrow.

I awaken with a plan. Well, several plans actually.

First, I'm going to call and make an appointment with my doctor. Tomorrow is technically two weeks, but I'm anxious to know that everything is okay. I have a date with Shay for dinner tonight, and hopefully some bedroom dessert. I manage to get an appointment right away. Apparently, they have gotten the report from the hospital, and agree that I need to be seen.

The next two plans, I formulate while I'm getting ready.

Second plan, talk to Laney. I know that Logan said not to, but I feel that she will listen to me, hopefully. I will call her from work later this afternoon. The third plan, is to call Shay's dad, and ask him to a game with the tickets that I have. I am not looking forward to this, but compared to what my friends are facing, this seems like a picnic. Time to man-up.

After I am showered and dressed, I send a quick text to Logan, letting him know that I will meet him at the club when I am done. I don't send one to Dante, because he will already be there. He is always there early. I don't think the guy believes in sleep. Maybe that will change if he ends-up with Lissa. I grab my wallet, keys, phone, and I am off.

I am sitting in the examination room in one of those gowns that tie at the front. I am holding it closed the best I can, but I still feel exposed. I hate wearing these things, and why do doctors always keep the rooms so cold? I swear they do it on purpose. Also, they all have cold fingers, like they have just stuck them in a freezer before coming in to examine you. Considering what part of my body those frozen fingers will be touching, I just might tell him to stick his hands under his armpits first. My penis is already trying to crawl up inside me from the cold room, there will be nothing to examine if the doctor tries to put his cold hands down there too.

There is a knock on the door, and then the doctor enters. He is a middle-aged man, with a little pot-belly and a balding head. He is on the short side, and what little hair he has is white. He reminds me of Santa Claus, minus the red suit and beard.

He pulls over a chair and sits in front of me. He has my chart in his hands, and after looking at it for a few more minutes, puts it on the table beside me.

"Well, son. I see that you have suffered from a penile fracture. Not as uncommon as you would think. It appears that there was concern about some tearing. Let's take a look at what is happening now."

Oh no, you don't! Before you put those hands anywhere near my junk, you are warming them up a bit, Santa.

"Can you warm your hands a bit first, please? It is a little cold in here."

He chuckles at me. "Not a problem, son. I will rub them together a bit to generate some warmth. Just open the gown, and relax."

Relax?

Not likely.

I slowly open the gown and expose myself to this man, under glaring lights, and a close-up view. I am not looking at him while he does this, so I concentrate on the diagram on the wall of the human body.

I jump slightly when I feel him touch me. He is making humming noises to himself and turning my penis around in hands, poking at various spots. I am concentrating hard on the diagram. I don't want to think about the fact that some guy is almost nose-to-penis with me, touching my dick, and *humming* what sounds like a show tune while he is doing it.

After what feels like an eternity, he finally releases his hold on me and leans back.

"Have you experienced an erection since the fracture?"

I make a sound in the back of my throat.

Almost non-stop since last week!

I am not going to tell him that though, so I just say, "I have had a few."

"Did you experience any pain, or difficulty maintaining it?"

"No."

"I have to ask, did you try ejaculating at all yet?"

This is beyond awkward.

I mumble, "Yes."

"I see. Was there any pain when you ejaculated? Any traces of blood in your semen?"

Shoot me now!

I shake my head in the negative.

"Have you any concerns about your recovery?'

Another shake of my head.

"Alright. From what I can see, and what you have told me, I don't believe that you had a tear big enough to be an issue. If the bruising and swelling went away in the time frame you were given, even with erections, and ejaculation, I would say that you are fine. If a problem was going to present itself, you would have experienced some negative signs by now. I would like for you to continue monitoring for signs of a problem, or if anything changes. Do you have any questions?"

Oh, thank you God!

I almost want to kiss the top of his bald, shiny head.

Almost.

My penis is going to be okay!

I look down at The Big Guy. He is looking very relaxed, like he knew it was going to go well for him.

I manage to say, "No. I think you answered them."

"Very good, then. I will put all this in your chart, and then you are free to get dressed. Please don't hesitate to call if you have questions or concerns that may arise."

"Thank you." I hope that tremble in my voice wasn't too noticeable, but he either doesn't hear it or chooses to ignore it.

He grabs my file and scribbles in it for a few moments. Then he bids me good day, and leaves me in the room to get dressed.

Once he is gone, I openly weep with relief while cradling my little champion to me. I make mental promises to never allow anything bad to happen to him again.

Only good times, will be had by all.

Chapter Twenty-Seven

I'm meeting the guys at the club.

I'm surprised to see Dante so relaxed around Logan. He must be better at this Cloak and Dagger stuff than I thought. You would never suspect the secrets he is keeping. They're both in the office when I get there, going over the plans for this week's theme, which is France. Our head chef will be in heaven. We have left the cuisine menu to him as he is French, after all. The music will be selected later by our DJ, and we have a band that covers popular French music coming in for Saturday. Most of our destinations we have done before. We just circulate the themes each week. It would be too costly to have a new one every week, and we would have to buy everything brand new each time. We have a list of twelve destinations that we use, and every once in a while we add a new one. If there is a holiday, we cater to that as well.

We spend most of our time together, working through the details for the weekend, but when three guys are together in a room, women and sex are bound to come-up.

"Hey, Logan. Did Alex tell you his news?"

Logan looks at me, and raises an eyebrow. I am not sure where Dante is going with this.

There are several newsworthy things that have happened, but I am not sure which one he is referring to.

Dante winks at me before saying, "He told Shayla that he loves her. Even more shocking though is that she claims to love him back."

Asshole.

Logan raises both his eyebrows now. "That is great. I am really happy for you both, but doesn't it seem a bit soon?"

I try to explain it to him. "It might be for others, but not for us. I have felt different with her right from the beginning, and it just feels right. She feels right. I want everything with her, and for her. I don't think about myself when I am with her, I am solely focused on her happiness. She is it. I don't want anyone else, I want her."

He looks doubtful, but I know now that it is stemming from his own past and it's not a judgment against me.

"Well, I can honestly say that I have never seen her happier," he says. "And you sure seem happy. I also have never heard you speak like that about a woman before, so I believe you feel what you are saying. Congratulations."

"Thanks. Did you know that she had a crush on me since she was a teenager?"

At this, he looks a little uncomfortable. "Not that I discuss these things with her, but yes, I was aware."

"Why did you never say anything?"

"What was I supposed to say? She was just a kid. I thought that she had outgrown it. Guess, I was wrong."

"Fair enough. Since we are talking about good things here, I have some other news." I pause here to make sure that I have attention all around. "The doctor said I am healed, and there will be no permanent, or lingering damage." Not his exact words, but close enough.

They both have huge smiles for me, and tell me how relieved they are to hear it. After the happy sentiments are passed around, Logan starts to look serious again. His next question takes all the air out of the room.

"I am a little concerned about my sister. My dad called me, because he went by her place to drop something off, and got no answer. Her neighbor said that she hasn't been home for a few weeks now. I called her, and she said she was staying with a friend, because her heat was being fixed. I don't know why I didn't believe her, but I didn't. I went by her place myself, and there is no sign of any work being done to her building, and there was no noise coming from her apartment."

Fuck, with a side of, fuck!

I intentionally keep my eyes away from Dante because I don't want to tip Logan off that we know anything. I ask him a question instead.

"Do you want me to ask Shay if she can give Lissa a call and make sure that she is okay?"

The look of relief on Logan's face makes me feel all kinds of guilty. I am hating Dante a little right now.

"That would be great, Alex. Thanks. I have enough to deal with without worrying about her as well. I love her to death, but keeping track of her is like trying to put a leash on a snake. She just slips right through, and goes her own way."

I chance a look at Dante.

He looks constipated.

Good. He deserves to feel tense about this.

What a mess!

Dante clears his throat. "What are we going to do about Shay's position opening-up?"

Logan looks thoughtful. "Well, I guess we can tell the staff that she had a better job offer somewhere else, and we will keep the position open in case we need to hire someone else."

"Sounds good." Dante looks to me, now. "Do you know when her last night will be?"

"She said her paper will be ready to hand in this week. I can ask her tonight, when she comes over for dinner."

Dante has a mischievous look in his eyes that should have warned me of his thoughts. "Planning on unleashing the full potential of your cock on her tonight?"

Logan screams like a girl, and covers his ears. "I don't want to hear this! I told you I didn't want to hear about you having sex with my cousin."

Dante is laughing now, and I have to chuckle a little myself. Logan looks like a nun who walked into a whorehouse.

Highly amusing.

I take pity on Logan, and tell Dante that I don't kiss and tell. He lets it go, because in the past, we all did.

I remember that I have two plans that I need to see through. I tell the guys that I need to make business calls. Not really, but they don't need to know.

They both say that they are done here for the day anyway and leave, saying that they will see me tomorrow.

Okay, now to make plan two happen.

I sit at the desk, where Logan just was, and look for Laney's number. When I find it, I take a deep breath before picking up the phone. This is either going to make things better, or worse.

I am hoping for better.

I listen to the phone ring twice, and then she answers.

"Hello?"

"Hi Laney, its Alex. How are you?"

There is a slight pause before she answers. "Fine, why?"

Great, I have to spell it out. "I heard about what happened at the restaurant."

"I just bet you did." She sounds snarky. I can't blame her.

"Logan came to see me right after you left him. He was a mess, Laney. You have to understand, that woman was from the night that he thought he had lost you."

"First, he never had me to lose. Second, there was more than that woman, on said night."

She had me there. Time to stop this train from crashing.

"I know, but in his defense, he doesn't even remember it." That made it sounds ten times worse.

Shit!

"What I meant, was that he was already drunk, and devastated before that happened. Honestly, I think they probably took advantage of him." That didn't sound better either.

She makes an angry sound, on the other end of the line. "Alex, just stop. I know that you are trying to defend your friend, and I can understand that. But please, just stop. He needs to do a lot of growing-up before I can risk any part of myself on him. Bad shit happens to all of us, it is how we choose to deal with it that defines us. His bullshit about being emotionally unavailable is just that, bullshit. You can clearly see that he was hurt badly once, but he can't let fear rule his life and just choose to bury his pain in women whenever something bad happens. I can't risk that he wouldn't do exactly that every time something didn't go his way if I was with him."

I am stunned.

I can't fix this. She is right, so right about all of it, but one thing. I know he would never be able to sleep around on her. I don't know what makes me so sure, I just know that it would never happen. I can't convince her of this though, so what can I say? I try anyway.

"I get that Laney, I do. I am just hoping that you can find some way to be his friend, at least. He is going to need one, and soon. But that is all I can say. I know that is asking a lot, given the way you feel, but I really do believe that he cares about you, and would never intentionally hurt you."

There is nothing on her end for quite some time. I fear that she hung-up on me, until I hear a sniffle.

Damn it! What did I say?

"I am not making any promises, but I will try. That's the best I can do, Alex. He has hurt me so much. I know he didn't know that he was hurting me, but he has. I just don't know how much more I can take, and if I let him in, he could destroy me."

Boy, that sounds just like what Logan said to me about his fears with Laney.

What a pair.

"I understand. Thank you, Laney. I am sorry that you are hurting. Is there anything that I can do?'

"Do you have a device that I can wire to his balls so that every time he does something stupid, I can just tap a button and make him suffer? Maybe a cock-clamp that I can squeeze on him?"

Ouch!

I actually grab my scepter and jewels in sympathy.

Laney has an evil streak. I will have to remember that.

"I don't, but how about I promise to dick-punch him if he makes you cry?'

She laughs, and I know that, for now, the storm has passed.

She agrees to let the other night go, but doesn't plan on making it too easy on Logan. She wants him to grovel. Hard woman, yet strangely exciting. Logan is going to be a lucky bastard if he doesn't screw this up. We end our call on a happier note, and I am smiling while patting myself on the back.

I am the man!

Now, to call Shay's dad.

I grab the phone and dial her parents' house. I wait for a few rings and then it goes to voicemail. I decide to hang up because I would rather ask in person, not over a machine.

With nothing left to do, I decide to call it a day and head home to get ready for my night with Shay.

☺

I have just gotten out of the shower, when I hear a text alert on my phone. Wrapping the towel around my hips, I move into the bedroom, grab my phone off the dresser, and see that it is from Shay.

Are we still on for dinner?

Silly woman. Not only are we still on, I have big plans for tonight. Heavy emphasis on the word, *big*.

Yes we are, what do you feel like eating?

Please say me!

> **Actually, I wanted to do the cooking. If that is okay?**

Okay? The thought of Shay cooking food for me, prepared by her own two hands, in my kitchen … well, the thought has caused some tenting to happen with my towel.

> **More than. Do you need me to pick anything up?**

> **I am stopping to grab what I will need. My treat tonight :)**

> **Well then, thank you. I am looking forward to it.**

> **I also have some news, and hopefully the answers to a few problems. Cya around 5?**

What problems is she referring to? Guess I will have to wait and hear about it all when she is here.

Five is perfect.

Cya then

That is three hours away, but it feels like an eternity. I put my phone back on the dresser and look down at myself. I will have to do something about this erection, otherwise I will be attacking her before she is properly in the door.

I still might.

Chapter Twenty-Eight

It is almost five.

My pulse is pounding in anticipation of the night ahead. I will have a beautiful woman cooking a meal for me and then I have special plans for desert.

My apartment is spotless, the kitchen has been prepped with everything that she might need, the wine is chilling, and I have candles lit in the living room with soft music playing in the background.

Romance is in the air.

There is a knock at the door, and my smile is probably predatory. I walk the short distance to the door and open it to reveal the woman of my heart's desire.

She has a long coat on, so I can't see what she is wearing, and she has paper bags in her arms with, I assume, the food. Her eyes, though, they are the most beautiful part of her, for they reveal the soul of the woman that has come to mean everything to me. I could stare into them forever, but I resist, and take the bags from her so that she can enter. She thanks me, and then glides inside.

Seeing this woman in my home is doing weird things to me. I feel myself holding my breath, as she walks around the living room. I want her to like my home. It shouldn't matter, really, but it does. A sense of longing comes over me so intense, it almost brings me to my knees. I want her in my home. I want to be able to wake-up beside her every morning, have coffee with her in the kitchen, come home to her after work, and spend all my moments sharing my life with her.

She gives me a playful look over her shoulder. "Are you going to put the groceries in the kitchen so you can take my coat?"

Shit!

I have been standing here, day-dreaming like an idiot. I quickly rush into the kitchen and deposit the bags on the counter. I rush back to the living room. She is standing just where I left her.

"Please forgive me, I found myself a little stupid at the sight of you in my home."

"Well, you are forgiven. Can I give you my coat?" She is smiling, but there is an impish glint to her eyes.

"Yes, of course. May I have your coat, Madame?"

"Madame, is it? I think I like that."

She begins to undo the buttons on her coat, and I am starting to sweat a bit. Something about the twinkle in her eyes, and the slow tease with the buttons, has me wondering what may, or may not, be under that coat. My breath is starting to pant slightly, and she hasn't even revealed anything yet.

Finally, she has reached the last button. She slowly lets the coat open, and then she shrugs it from her shoulders.

Jesus!

She has on nothing but a pair of thigh-high stockings with killer, black heels; black lace lingerie; and, God help me, an apron. The apron is black and white, just like a French maid would wear.

My tongue feels too thick for my mouth, and it is not the only thing that feels too thick to be confined. My eyes must be bugging out of my head, but I can't help it. She is a walking dream, right out of my kitchen fantasies. I know that I said I wanted to see her in an apron, but this is beyond anything even my dirty mind could conjure. I am now having visions of kitchen porn, playing out in my head. I am trying to tell her how amazing she looks, but all that I am managing is choking and wheezing sounds.

Embarrassing, much?

She takes pity on me, and walks over. "I can see that you are not in any shape to take my coat, so if you would just point me to where I can put it?" The little minx is enjoying this, as she is trying not to laugh at my stupefied state.

I point to the coat-rack behind the front door. She sashays over to the rack, and makes a production out of stretching to hang it on the top arm. Her calves are emphasized by the motion, and her legs seem even longer. I notice that from the back, the bottom part of her lingerie barely hides the firm globes of her ass. I make a strangled sound over this discovery, and she looks at me over her shoulder.

She looks very smug about the effect she is having on me.

She had better be careful, or the only thing being eaten tonight will be her.

She finishes hanging her coat, and then strolls casually through to the kitchen. Like a puppy, I follow her. She is at the counter, taking items out of the bags. From what I can tell, it looks like we are having Italian tonight.

Yum!

She asks for specific pans and utensils, and then she proceeds to start the prep work for dinner. She tells me that we are having chicken cacciatore, with a spinach salad, and her own salad dressing. I have three specific parts of my body at war here. My mouth is watering at what she has just described, my heart is warmed by having her cook for me, and my dick is kicking in my pants to be let loose on her.

Pretty soon, she has things simmering and the aroma wafting around my kitchen is nothing short of heavenly. I kept offering to help, and she gently, but firmly refused each time. She has finished with the salad, and is now pouring flour into a bowl and measuring other ingredients. I didn't notice the flour before, and now I am anxious to see what she is doing.

"What are you making now?"

"Oh, I forgot to mention that I am going to bake some homemade bread to go with the meal as well."

No. Way.

Shay is going to bake for me. Shay is going to be bent over my oven. Shay is wearing an apron. It is my kitchen fantasy!

She begins to knead the dough, and I almost fall off the stool. Her breasts are being lifted, and squeezed together with the motion. I must whimper, which she takes as a sign that I am getting hungry, and promises that it will be ready soon.

If she only knew.

She molds the bread into a pan, and takes it to the oven.

Then she does it.

She opens my oven door, and bends down.

I. Loose. My. Mind.

I don't remember how I managed to do it, but from one moment to the next, I have her pinned against the wall.

I am holding her head in my hands, and I am devouring her mouth. She is kissing me back and digging her nails into my shoulders. My pelvis is grinding into her, and I am trying to be gentle, but I fear I am failing. Not that she seems to mind. She is arching her back, and I slide one leg between her parted thighs. She begins to rub herself against my leg, and is making desperate little noises in the back of her throat.

I snap.

So does her lingerie, as I rip it at the juncture of her body.

I slide my hand between her thighs and find her soaking wet. More than ready for what I am about to unleash.

I pop the button on my pants and yank at the fly. I find myself through my boxers, and release my throbbing cock.

Without breaking the kiss, I grab her legs and wrap them around my waist. I then line us up, and thrust into her wet, heat in one, glorious stroke right to the hilt.

She breaks the kiss to let out a strangled scream. I would have worried that I hurt her, but her heels are digging into my ass, urging me on. I pull out almost completely, and slam back in, swiveling my hips as I do. This time it is me making the noises. She is so tight and silky around me that my eyes are rolling back in my head. It's amazing, the way her body feels squeezing me in rhythmic pulses. I take a deep breath and begin to really move. I am pounding her into the wall, but that only seems to excite her more. She has a tight grip on my hair and is meshing her mouth back with mine.

Yes!

I change the angle slightly and slide in deeper. We both groan through the kiss. I am grinding myself into her now, and I must be reaching a part deep inside of her that seems to be her sweet spot. She is clawing at my back and groaning louder. I keep hitting that spot for her and she doesn't last long. She wrenches her lips from mine, and she shatters around me. I am in awe of just how beautiful she is in her release. I want to put that look on her face again, and again. Unfortunately, The Big Guy has other plans, and I am having my own orgasm on the heels of hers. I feel light-headed from the pleasure, and I press myself against her to stop us from sliding down the wall.

We are panting and breathless, covered in a light sweat.

It feels glorious.

I gentle my hold on her, and she gingerly untangles her legs from around me. I lower her to the floor, and put my arms around her, just holding her close to my pounding heart. I kiss the top of her head.

"Sorry about that. You have no idea what the sight of you in my kitchen was doing to me. Then you bent over my oven and, well, I had to have you."

She smiles at me. "Don't ever apologize for something like that. You can ravage me anytime you want."

"Careful, or I will take you at your word, and who knows when the mood might strike me. I don't think you would want to find yourself bent over the meat counter at the grocery store."

She bursts out laughing.

I show her to the bathroom, so that she can clean-up. I walk into my bedroom so I can clean myself too, in my bathroom. I also get her a pair of shorts, since I ruined her lingerie. I knock on the guest bathroom door, and wait for her to open it. She smiles, rather sheepishly and takes the shorts from me.

Adorable.

☺

Dinner was delicious.

Shay created one of the most amazing meals that I have had the pleasure of eating. The bread was so light and fluffy, it was like a buttery cloud in my mouth. I think I might have had a tear in my eye while I was eating it. I told you that I missed having someone bake for me. There is nothing better than fresh-from-the-oven, baked goods. I was spoiled growing up with a mother who loved to bake. I am looking forward to having a woman baking for me again.

We chatted through our meal about her article. She was really excited about it, and even offered to let me read it. I told her how proud I was of her, and that seemed to be the right thing to say, for she ended-up in my lap for some lip service.

Once dinner was finished, we both cleaned the kitchen, and even had a bubble fight with the suds from the sink. I can't remember the last time I had so much fun doing dishes. We agreed to take our wine into the living room. I sat on the couch, and she curled herself into me like a contented cat.

We are snuggling, and she is smiling up at me, but then seems to remember something.

"Oh, I almost forgot to tell you about the solution to some of our problems." She starts to play with a button on my shirt, as she talks. "I had coffee with Elisabeth this morning. First, she told me about the stalker. Poor thing, I wish I had known. Not that I could have done anything, but at least she would have had someone to talk to about it. Anyways, she is terrified of going back to her apartment alone. I am looking for a temporary place to stay, while I move out of my parents' home, and until they get used to the idea of us living together. So the solution is, I am going to live with her until she feels more secure, and the time is right for me to move in here. What do you think?"

I feel a huge smile blooming on my face. It is perfect. It solves our problem with her parents, for now, and it will also save Dante's ass, for now. A win-win.

I grab her face and kiss her.

My woman is a genius!

She pulls away gently, and giggles. "I am taking that as a sign that you like the idea?"

"Like it? Are you kidding me? I love it! Anything that gets you in my home sooner, is awesome. The fact that it also gets Lissa out of Dante's place before Logan finds out, is a bonus. You, my dear, are amazing."

"I can't take all the credit. It was Lissa's idea as well. Oh, and Dante should definitely make a play for her, but after she is back at her own place. She has had a crush on him for about as long as I had one on you."

That floors me. How did we not know that we had secret admirers in Logan's family?

Oh, right. It was Logan's family, and he was keeping that to himself. Not that I blame him, too much. He must have felt awkward hearing about his sister, and his cousin, crushing on his friends.

Still, it could have been mentioned when they were of age.

Just saying.

"He will be very happy to hear that. The downer in all this is, Logan. What are we going to do about that?"

"We are not doing anything. That is between the three of them. Honestly though, I don't see why it should matter to Logan. Besides, at least he knows that Dante is a good guy. She could do a lot worse, and has."

"I agree, but he isn't logical when it comes to Lissa. He has always been very protective of her."

"Too protective of her, if you ask me. He stifles her, and she doesn't know how to tell him without hurting him. She is almost twenty five years old, and he treats her like she is still a child. You realize that by smothering her, she has had to hide a lot from him, and it has also made her rebel in ways that he is definitely not going to like if he finds out"

"What do you mean? What has she done?"

"Nope, not my place to say anything. Just warning you, because when Logan realizes the extent of what he has done to her, he is going to need you."

"Okay, you are starting to scare me."

"No, don't be scared. She hasn't done anything illegal, or nefarious. She just felt that she had to push back at him, in her own ways, even if he didn't know it."

I am rubbing my forehead with my thumb, realizing that when Logan gets wind of all this, plus Dante, well, we should probably all chip in to have a nice padded room ready for him.

"God, I can't imagine what this is going to do to him."

"It is not for us to worry about. All we can do is be here for him when he needs us. I am sure in the end, everything will be fine. Have some faith, Alex."

"Have you met, Logan?"

She snorts at this. "Yes, he needs to get that pickle out of his ass. Maybe this will dislodge it."

I snort with her, and then we are both laughing.

I drag her onto my lap, and wrap my arms around her.

We stop laughing around the same time, and just stare into each other's eyes. I reach up, and tuck a stray hair behind her ear. I caress the shell of it with my fingers, and then trail them down the column of her neck.

The apron came off before we ate. I didn't think that I could eat while she sat across from me, sitting in her apron, reminding me of kitchen sex. I gave her a t-shirt, since all she had on under the apron was my shorts, and her lingerie. I am stroking the skin of her collarbone, exposed above the neck of the shirt. I am looking into her eyes, and watching them begin to darken.

I move to the edge of the couch, and with one arm under her legs, while holding her to me, I stand. I am done talking about my friends and their problems. She snuggles into my arms with a contented sigh. I walk towards my bedroom.

It is time for dessert.

Chapter Twenty-Nine

We agree to meet at Destinations the following afternoon so that she can formally tell Logan that she is finished.

I spent two hours enjoying my dessert last night. The Big Guy performed like an athlete. She had to go home afterwards, much to my disappointment. When she explained that she wanted to respect her parents, and to convince them that I was an honorable man, I couldn't fault her logic. She also wanted to have breakfast with her parents and let them know that she was going to be moving in with Lissa. I hoped it went well, for all our sakes.

I am at the club, lounging at the bar, talking to Dante.

"So, now that her article is done, when do they publish it?"

"The magazine runs monthly, so it will be in next month's issue. Why, do you read the magazine?"

"Fuck, no! That is a girly magazine. I was just asking. Besides, I know that Lissa reads it, so if I wanted to see Shayla's article, I could just have her show me."

"You seem to know quite a bit about her these days. Living together must be an eye-opener."

"Living with who is an eye-opener?"

I whip my head around at the sound of Logan's voice.

Fuuuuck!

We didn't even see him approach. Where are Dante's ninja skills? Why didn't he see him, or hear him.

I chance a quick look back to Dante, but the guy is gone!

What the hell?

He must have ducked behind the bar.

I turn to face, Logan. He looks like shit. His hair is rumpled, and he is sporting a 5:00 shadow. His clothes aren't wrinkled, but I would bet that he slept in them. Either Laney hasn't spoken to him yet, or she is really making him grovel.

"Oh, I was just thinking aloud, about living with Shay. It is going to be an eye-opener."

Logan grabs the back of his neck and starts to rub. "Well, I wouldn't bank on that happening too soon. I just spoke to Lissa, and she told me that Shay is going to be living with her."

"Yes, she told me, but that is only until her parents are on board with her living with me."

"Lissa is really excited about having her there. It will be good for her to have someone around to keep an eye on her."

Okay, now I am getting a bit steamed. Lissa doesn't need a keeper, and my woman is not a babysitter!

"Logan, she is a grown woman, capable of living her own life. When are you going to let her live it?"

Now he is the one who looks steamed. "Don't talk to me like you know what is best for her."

"I am not assuming that I know what is best for her, I am just suggesting that maybe she should be the judge of that."

Some of the anger drains from him. "You're right, but it is just so damned hard to let go. After my mom died, my dad fell apart. I was the one who looked after her. I have been doing it for fifteen years. I don't know if I will ever be able to stop looking after her."

"Maybe it's time that you let her try to find someone else who can."

"What is that supposed to mean? Like a guy?" He sounds angry again.

"Maybe, if that is what will make her happy. It would take some of the weight off of you."

"No man is ever going to love her the way she deserves, or care for her the way she needs."

"You said that about Shay too, and I would like to think that I am the man that can give her all that she deserves and needs."

Logan looks really hard at me. "Do you know something?"

Shit, fuck, and goddammit!

How do I look him in the eye, and lie?

Dante, you suck!

"All I am saying, is that you were wrong about me, and Shay. Maybe Lissa can be happy too."

"She is happy, she doesn't need a man to make her happy."

"Have you asked her?"

"If she needs a man to make her happy?"

"No, if she is happy."

You could see the guilt wash over his face. "No, I haven't."

"Maybe you should."

One side of his mouth tips up in a half-smile. "When did you become, Freud? Seems my brilliant cousin is making you smarter."

"No arguing there. I told you, she has made me want to be a better man."

He nods his head, and then scans the bar. "Where is Dante? Usually he is here already."

Oh he is, just not where Logan can see him.

Jerk.

"Maybe he is the control room?"

"Okay, I'll go and see if he is there. We need to finalize everything for tonight. Thanks, Alex. I will talk to her."

I slap him on the back, and he walks off towards the corridor leading to the computer rooms. I wait until he is out of sight, then I round the bar.

Sure enough, there is my hulking friend, crouched into a little ball under the counter. I don't know if it the sight of him under there, or the stress, but

I burst out laughing. He slowly slinks out, scowling at me. It just makes me laugh harder. He peeks his head up, resembling a gopher. Now I am doubled over, in complete hysterics. Once Dante is satisfied that Logan is gone, he stands up. He is just standing there glaring at me. I now have tears running down my cheeks, and am having trouble breathing.

Dante heaves a sigh. "I don't know what you find so funny. That was too close. My balls still haven't dropped back down."

I manage to get some control of myself. He is right. That was too close, and I am getting tired of it.

"You need to tell him."

"Are you insane? Besides, there isn't anything to tell. Nothing has happened."

"Hmmm….but you want something to happen. Which reminds me, Shay said that you have the green light, as soon as she is back at her own place, its game-on."

He stops scowling, and a huge smile brightens his face. "Yeah?"

"Yes. Now, the right thing to do would be to tell your best friend that you plan on dating his sister."

"I know you're right, but I don't want this to cause a rift between us. We aren't just friends, we work together too."

"Yes, it might be tense at first, but he will eventually get over it. Ultimately, he wants Lissa to be happy. He can't hold a grudge forever, or it will put a wall between them, and that I can guarantee, he won't let happen."

"It would help if he was in a better mood. Given the way he is acting these days, I can't see it going over well."

"I am working on it. Just promise me that you won't wait much longer. I hate all this lying."

"Deal. So what are you working on to get his gloomy mood lifted?"

"Laney. She is the key to his moods. As long as she is happy with him, he will be happy."

"Huh, makes sense. I just wish he would stop making excuses, and just go after her. Anyone can see the way they feel about each other, except apparently themselves."

"That is what we need to work on. They have both been made aware of how the other feels, now we just need to make sure that Logan doesn't screw it all up."

"We?"

"Yes we, Tonto."

"Hey, why am I Tonto? I want to be The Lone Ranger."

"You are already James Bond, you don't get to be another cool guy. So, let's go, sidekick, before he comes back. Once he realizes you're not in the computer rooms, and sees you standing here, he'll be back in our faces. We'll go to the office and say you were in there."

"You are getting pretty good at lying, you know."

"Shut-up, Tonto, or you will get downgraded to the horse."

He shut-up.

☺

We are all in the office when Shay arrives.

She knocks on the door and then enters the room.

I will never get used to the way seeing her affects me. My heart rate increases, my breathing speeds up, and my penis gets happy in my pants.

She smiles at me, but then turns her attention to Logan. He gets up from where he was sitting behind the desk and walks over to enfold her in a hug. You can see how much they care about each other. I have a small family, with no siblings, and a few distant cousins that I never see. They pull apart, but they are smiling at each other. Logan steps back, and indicates that she can sit at the desk.

She shakes her head. "This won't take long. I have a formal letter for you to put on file. It states that I am no longer available to work for you. I wasn't sure how you wanted to handle this. I am assuming that it needs to be all legal, since I was employed here on the books, and received pay for the shifts that I worked. I can't thank you enough for allowing me to work here."

"You were an excellent waitress, and you don't need to thank me. How did the article turn out?"

"My editor loved it. She said that it was honest and real. She said that readers are going to be able to really connect with it."

"I am glad we could help then. What are your plans now?"

"I am going to keep writing my monthly articles, but I think I might try doing some freelance work as well."

"That is great. I am sure that you will be a success at whatever you put your mind to. I hear that you are moving in with Lissa?"

Dante and I have been passively watching and listening, but at the mention of Lissa, we both pay closer attention to the conversation.

Shay smiles warmly at Logan. "Yes, and I am really looking forward to it. She is doing me a huge favor, and I can't thank her enough."

"She is really excited about it. It's the first time that she has sounded happy in a few weeks."

Ouch! Dante doesn't look happy about that.

I am sure that she was stressed over the stalker, and trying to keep Logan from becoming suspicious by being vague and evasive when she was talking to him. He just took it to mean that she was less than happy.

"I know that we will have a lot of fun together, and raise some hell as well."

Logan is looking edgy after that last comment. Time to change the subject.

"Why don't we all head out and celebrate all the good things that are happening. We have some time before we need to start prepping for tonight. Let's go to our usual pub. We can get a bite to eat, and raise a glass together."

Dante nods his head, and Logan can't refuse the hopeful smile Shay is aiming at him.

"Okay, but let me give Lissa a call. She might want to meet us since we are celebrating something good for her too."

Logan turns his back, and starts to dial his phone so he doesn't see the panic that has descended on the rest of us. We are all staring at each other with varying degrees of horror on our faces.

Shit.

Chapter Thirty

We are sitting at our favorite pub, but it is anything but relaxed.

Logan seems to be ignorant to the tension, which is a good thing. The rest of us feel like we are on a train that is about to crash.

We have all ordered a drink, but we are waiting for Lissa to arrive before we order the food.

Yes, she is coming, much to our mutual dread.

Dante looks beyond constipated, he looks like his bowels may never work again. The guy is a wreck.

Shay has been managing to keep Logan engaged in conversation, but keeps shooting me looks of panic.

Me? I feel like I am going to be sick.

The bell chimes above the door, and we all swivel our heads in unison.

I have mentioned before about Lissa's kind of beauty, but really, it is ethereal. She truly resembles a walking Barbie. She is tall and slender, with long golden-blond hair, and big, bright blue eyes. As I have also mentioned before, he breasts are spectacular. I am sorry if that seems wrong of me to say, but I would be dead not to notice. She is wearing white capris with a red, fitted blouse, and white sandals with ties that cross over her ankles. She carries herself like a beauty queen, and leaves a trail of panting men in her wake. The genes that she and Logan share should be used for science. People would pay millions to have a tenth of their beauty.

She smiles at us as she approaches, and if I wasn't sitting beside Dante, I would not have heard his rumble. It is more like the noise that a jungle cat makes when it is purring.

Logan is out of his chair, and sweeping her up in a big ol' bear hug. She squeals, but then starts laughing, and hugs him back. He puts her down, and then pulls her chair out for her. She thanks him, and takes her seat. She reaches over, and snags Shay's hand off the table.

"I can't wait for you to move in. How did Uncle Mike and Auntie take the news?"

I am anxious to hear this as well, since we haven't had a chance to talk about it.

Shay shifts a bit in her seat. "Mom was super supportive, as I expected. Dad, well, he reacted pretty much like I expected too."

Lissa gives her a sympathetic look. "That bad?"

"Well, it could have gone better. Let's just say that my mother will have her work cut out for her, calming him down. Honestly though, even with him being upset, it hasn't put a damper on how excited I am."

"Me too. We are going to have so much fun. Remember how we always talked about having our own place together when we were younger?"

Shay chuckles. "I remember. We would dream about all the adventures that we would have, and of course, all the boys."

Lissa giggles.

Logan looks like his pickle just got wedged further up his ass.

Dante is scowling.

I clear my throat. "Lissa needs a drink so that we can make a toast."

There have been two waiters hovering on the fringes, just waiting for this very opportunity. They both rush over, and there may have been some shoving to reach her first. I have to admit, the one guy had some serious moves and totally blocked the other guy, who is now glaring daggers into the back of his head. Lissa gives her drink order to the waiter beside her, but it is the other guy who rushes off to get it. Within a matter of moments, the guy rushes back with her drink, and presents it to her as if he were serving the queen. The guy who took her order is looking murderous. It is all highly entertaining.

Logan raises his glass. "To Lissa, and Shay on their new living arrangements. May God have mercy on us all."

The women roll their eyes, but Dante and I chuckle over this. We all raise our glasses, and clink. I did notice the look that passed between Lissa and Dante when they clinked their glasses together, and let's just say that it is a good thing that Logan wasn't watching. Even I felt a little singed from the heat. The two waiters are still standing by our table, so we give them our orders.

The conversation is surprisingly easy, and Logan seems oblivious to the undercurrents at the table. Lissa is telling us all about a new job that she has for some expensive penthouse uptown. She is an interior designer, and is really good at it, and she is in high demand for her work. Shay tells everyone a little about what she put in the article, and which parts she wrote based on information that she acquired from working at the club. Dante, Logan and I just relax and listen. I am actually having a pleasant time. I can feel the tension draining from me, and I know that Dante is feeling the same.

The food arrives, and conversation becomes a bit slower as we eat. I keep sneaking glances at Shay. We both have to be back to work soon, and as much as I am enjoying this, I want to spend some time with her alone.

I lean towards her and whisper in her ear, "How about we finish our meal, and leave these three to their fate. I have something that I want to give you."

She raises an eyebrow and smiles at me. "Didn't you give it to me enough last night?"

Naughty girl.

"It is never enough with you, and I have something else to give you. But if you want, I could give you both."

"Really? Here in the restaurant?"

"You did say that I can ravage you anytime. I believe that I warned you not to say that."

She snorts. "Shall I bend over the table now? I don't think that dinner and a show is what everyone here might want though."

I chuckle under my breath. I love her sass. "Okay, I will agree with you there. Can you take a walk with me, before you have to go back to work?"

"That, I can do."

We announce to the table that we are going to take a walk before heading back. Dante looks absolutely panic stricken, but Lissa just waves us off, and gives Shay a wink.

"You two love-birds go on. I will call you later, Shay to fix all the details for when you are moving in. Nice to see you again, Alex. I guess I will be seeing a lot of you, if Shay is going to be living with me."

"It was nice to see you too, Lissa. I imagine you will be seeing me quite a bit now, at least until I can convince Shay to move-in with me instead."

Lissa just giggles, and says goodbye to us.

Logan says that he will see me at the office later, and asks if I can grab coffee for all us on the way back. I agree and say that I will see him there.

Dante just throws a wave at us over his shoulder. He is too busy staring at his plate, like the answers to his problems might be there. I should feel guilty for leaving him like this, but I am still angry enough at him about the lying, that I don't.

I throw some money down on the table to cover our bill, take Shay's hand, and we are out the door. She is giggling beside me as we start walking down the street.

"What is so funny?"

"Did you see the look on Dante's face when we said we were leaving? He reminded me of a child being left at school for the first time. Parts fear, anxiety, and abandonment. Poor guy."

"Don't go feeling sorry for the guy. He did this to himself, and dragged us all into it with him. I had to lie to Logan today. I am not happy about that."

"I know, but really, how else could he have handled it? Would you have done anything differently?"

"Yes, no, maybe. I don't know, but he needs to come clean. The longer he keeps this from the Logan, the worse it is going to be when he finds out."

"I agree, but it is not our decision to make. Maybe I can suggest that Lissa talks to him instead of Dante. He might take it better coming from her, because let's face it, he would never be mad at her, and would do anything to make her happy, even though he refuses to stop treating her like a child, and trying to control her."

"I tried talking to him today about that. Hopefully I gave him some things to think about. Maybe you are right, and Lissa should be the one to tell him."

"I will talk to her about it. Now, what did you want to give me?"

I don't want to do this on the street. There is a little garden park a block away, which I am heading for.

"All in good time. I thought maybe we could sit at the park?"

She smiles. "That sounds nice."

It only takes about five more minutes to reach the gardens. There are benches between flower sections, so I choose a nice sunny spot, and lower myself, tugging her onto my lap. She laughs at the unexpected move, but snuggles herself against me. I wrap my arms around her, and just enjoy the way she feels. She is the most incredible thing that has ever happened to me, and I still need moments to just feel her close to me and absorb how lucky I am. I can't believe how much she has changed my life and what I think about myself. She is my oasis, and I never knew how parched I was until she came into my life.

I give her a gentle squeeze, and then release one of my arms from around her, so that I can reach into my pocket.

No, it is not what you are thinking. I know things have happened fast for us, but not that fast!

I take her hand and put a key in it.

She looks at me questioningly.

I explain. "I know that you will be living with Lissa, but I want you to know that my door is always open to you. I wanted to show you how serious I am about wanting you to be in my home, and in my life."

She smiles tenderly at me, and I can see that her eyes are a bit misty.

My own eyes might be a bit misty too.

She closes her hand around the key, and then leans in and gently brushes her lips against mine. I close my eyes to savor the sensation of her lips melting against my own. I reach up with one hand, and cradle the back of her head. I nibble at her lower lip and tug slightly, encouraging her to let me in. She sighs into my mouth, while parting her lips. I seal our lips together and begin to mate my tongue with hers. I am aware that we are in a public park, and that this needs to remain P.G. Good thing she is on my lap, for there is nothing family-friendly going on down there.

I slowly end the kiss and pull back to look into her eyes. I have said before how gorgeous her eyes are, but they are especially so when they are full of love for me.

She reaches up and traces the line of my jaw while saying, "Thank-you for the key. I am looking forward to the day that it truly becomes the key to my home."

"I love you, Shay. You are all I want. I will wait for as long as you need."

"I am only going to stay with Lissa until my dad can handle another blow. Once he gets over the fact that I am not under his roof anymore, it will be easier to tell him that I am moving in with you."

"Like I said, take all the time you need. As long as I know that you are mine, I can wait."

"I love you, Alex. You are the best thing that has ever happened to me."

She wraps her arms around me, and lays her head on my shoulder.

I put my arms around her, and whisper into her ear, "I was just thinking the same thing."

Epilogue

Three months later …..

I am sitting beside Shay's dad at the soccer game. I would like to say that we have become close, but that would be a lie. I would say that we tolerate each other for Shay's sake. I will never be enough for her in his eyes, but then he isn't going to be my favorite person either.

I wore a jock strap, and a cup to the game.

Shay is now living with me, and I couldn't be happier. Her dad on the other hand…well, happy is not the word I would use. Shay thought that going to the game together might help mend the fences that I apparently broke by taking his little girl away from him and corrupting by making her live in sin with me. So here I am, sitting beside a man that could crush me physically, and legally.

Her dad's team scores a goal, and he launches himself from the seat, taking ten years off my life in the process. I wasn't paying attention to the game, and for a moment, I thought he was getting ready to attack me.

I might have even peed a little.

Her dad looks down at me, and I know that I am cowering, but my fear has me immobilized.

"Oh, for fuck's sake boy, I am not going to hurt you." He is smiling though, and it is decidedly evil. "I might help hide the evidence if you disappear, but I won't hurt you."

I feel the blood drain from my face.

He must notice, because he sighs and then sits back down beside me. "Look, all joking aside, I don't want you to fear me. I like it, but Shay doesn't, and her happiness is my priority. For some reason, she seems to think that you make her happy. I have to admit, she appears happy, and you are not as horrible a choice as she could have made."

"Thank you, I think."

"I still don't approve of her living with you, though. A young woman shouldn't be living with a man, at least not until there is a ring on her finger, and maybe a pre-nup."

"If I put a ring on her finger, would you approve?"

He looks at me sharply. "Why would you do that? Just to buy my approval?"

I take a deep breath.

Here goes nothing. "No sir, I would not do that to gain your approval. I would do it because I love your daughter. Her happiness is my priority every day, and will be for the rest of my days. I want to share every smile with her, and hope that I helped put it there. I want to grow old with the love of my life, your daughter."

He is still assessing me, and I fear that I just made a huge mistake.

Will he warn me, before I disappear?

He finally smiles. Or what I assume is his version of a smile. It is just a slight curling of his lips, and little crinkling around his eyes.

"Well, now that is more like it. You sounded like a man just now, not a mouse. We both agree that her happiness is what is important here. I respect you for saying that to me. I know that I have been hard on you, but maybe I can ease off a bit. Does this mean that you will make an honest woman of her?"

"Yes sir, that is what I am saying. If I wasn't worried about it being too soon, I would have asked you for her hand before now. So, I am asking you now, may I have your daughter's hand in marriage, sir?"

He looks thoughtful for a moment, and then says, "No."

No?

After I just put myself through all that, he said, "*No?*"

I almost miss it, but there is a twinkle in his eyes now.

He hold his hand out to me, in the way men do for a handshake. I hesitantly put my hand in his. He is actually smiling now, a real one.

"I am just teasing you, Alex. If my daughter agrees when you ask her, then you have my blessing."

The relief I feel is overwhelming.

He gives my hand a final squeeze, not gently either, and then removes it. We have a mutual understanding of each other, and resume watching the game.

I wish that the path that lead to this moment could have been smoother, but then the outcome might have been different, so really, I wouldn't change a thing. If you think the path I travelled was rough, Dante and Logan had it just as bad, if not worse in some aspects, but that is their story to tell, not mine.

As for me?

I am spending the rest of my life with the woman that I love.

My name is Alex Bradley, and this was my story.

P.S. She said yes.

The End

Acknowledgements

I would like to thank all the people that helped this book come to fruition.

I want to say a special thanks to the following people: To my husband and children, who suffered with me through my struggles, continued to encourage me and share in my accomplishments. To my sister who believed in me, and kept reminding me that I could do this. To my in-laws and friends, who supported me, and listened to me. To my best-friend, who has been reading my stories since we were teens. To my mother, who taught me what it means to reach for a dream, and always saw the best in me. I know that she is watching me from heaven, and I still feel her endless love and devotion.

I want to mention some others who have helped me along the way. Author Layla Stevens and author Jean Oram for all your advice, Nicole Johnson and Christine Bowden for your valuable feedback on my book, Author C. E. Black for holding my hand through the final steps and Neeley Bratcher for her wonderful work editing my book.

Thank you to everyone for helping to make my dream come true. I couldn't have done this without you.

About The Author

S. H. Timmins lives in Ontario, Canada with her husband and three children. She has always had a passion for reading, and is a self-proclaimed bookie.

You can find her on Facebook

https://www.facebook.com/S.H.Timmins.author

Made in the USA
Charleston, SC
12 August 2015